"Look out!" w

Legs tangled, arms flailed, and a second later, Joanna was sprawled on the firm mattress with Callahan spread over top of her.

The cool air from the AC on her bare feet made her shiver—or was that from the heat from the heavy length of Ben's body that was burning into hers?

"Um," she said, licking her lips and looking up at him. He didn't move. She didn't ask him to. He felt good.

"Don't do that," he said, his breath sounding a little short.

"Don't do what?"

"Lick your lips like that."

"Oh, sorry," she said, not sounding sorry at all.

"I should probably get up," he said, his breath warm on her cheek. "But I really don't want to."

His words, his touch were pushing her too close to the edge.

And resisting temptation had never been one of her strong suits.

Dear Reader,

Straight to the Heart offered me the chance to write about my favorite of all law enforcement characters, the U.S. marshal. In this book, U.S. marshal Joanna Wyatt is the sister of Texas Ranger Jarod Wyatt, the hero from my American Heroes Blaze, *Hard to Resist.* Joanna was raised by two strong Texan men: her dad and her brother. And she's definitely carrying on her family tradition. It was a pleasure to get to know Joanna, a strong, alpha woman, and to find her romantic match.

But what kind of hero would be right for such a heroine? Well, Ben Callahan, cowboy and former SEAL, suddenly appeared and fit the bill. He's perfect for Joanna, and she for him, though romance isn't easy for two strong people with similar personalities. Opposites may attract, but in my opinion, these two set off a lot more sparks on the way to their happily-ever-after.

Straight to the Heart was a fun book to write, and I hope you enjoy it. Let me know on Twitter, Facebook, Harlequin.com or email me at samhunter@samanthahunter.com.

Thanks for reading,

Samantha Hunter

Samantha Hunter

STRAIGHT TO THE HEART

TORONTO NEW YORK LONDON
AMSTERDAM PARIS SYDNEY HAMBURG
STOCKHOLM ATHENS TOKYO MILAN MADRID
PRAGUE WARSAW BUDAPEST AUCKLAND

ISBN-13: 978-0-373-79663-2

STRAIGHT TO THE HEART

This edition published by arrangement with Harlequin Books S.A.

For questions and comments about the quality of this book please contact us at Customer_eCare@Harlequin.ca.

www.Harlequin.com

Printed in U.S.A.

ABOUT THE AUTHOR

Samantha Hunter lives in Syracuse, New York, where she writes full-time for Harlequin Books. When she's not plotting her next story, Sam likes to work in her garden, quilt, cook, read and spend time with her husband and their dogs. Most days you can find Sam chatting on the Harlequin Blaze boards at Harlequin.com, or you can check out what's new, enter contests or drop her a note at her website, www.samanthahunter.com.

Books by Samantha Hunter

HARLEQUIN BLAZE

142—VIRTUALLY PERFECT
173—ABOUT LAST NIGHT...
224—FASCINATION*
229—FRICTION*
235—FLIRTATION*
267—HIDE & SEEK*
299—UNTOUCHED
343—PICK ME UP
365—TALKING IN YOUR SLEEP...
478—HARD TO RESIST**
498—CAUGHT IN THE ACT
542—MAKE YOUR MOVE
584—I'LL BE YOURS FOR CHRISTMAS
620—MINE UNTIL MORNING

*The HotWires
**American Heroes

Thanks to Kathryn Lye for her encouragement on the initial idea and while writing this book, and to the Harlequin staff overall for all of their hard work and support on every project.

To Jeannie Watt and Kari Dell, who were so generous with their time helping this New York writer get a handle on Western life, cowboys and roadhouses.

As always, my love to Mike.

Prologue

"YOU THINK HE'S COVERING FOR someone?" U.S. Marshal Joanna Wyatt set the file down on her boss's desk, meeting Don's eyes squarely. She had no idea why he was asking her about his case—the murder of a rodeo official by an organized-crime thug—but maybe he needed to brainstorm ideas. The cowboy who had witnessed the murder wasn't cooperating, but that wasn't her problem. She was impatient, wanting to know about her own status and her next assignment.

"That or he's being threatened. Someone might have gotten to him, scared him. That would explain why he refused to come into protective custody, didn't want to leave his family exposed. But he also rejected the idea of a protective detail. Said he could handle it himself," Don responded, sounding tired.

Joanna pursed her lips, grabbing the report and scanning it again. Former navy SEAL, covert ops, cowboy. She knew the type. She'd been raised by two men with similar backgrounds, her father and brother, both Texans, both Texas Rangers. Ben Callahan's response to protective custody didn't shock her; a man like that tended to face his trouble head-on.

"I imagine he's probably not afraid of much, and he probably *could* handle it himself," she acknowledged. "This guy must have some serious skills, and friends who might back him up."

Don scowled. "That may be, but he doesn't have the jurisdiction nor the blessing of the U.S. government to do so. He's a civilian now."

"Why refuse a personal detail?" Joanna mused aloud.

"He said having bodyguards would draw more attention to him, that strangers would stand out like sore thumbs, raise flags."

"He's probably right. Texas towns are tight-knit communities. Everyone knows everyone, no exceptions."

Don glared. Joanna shrugged. She couldn't help it if Callahan was right.

"So what are you going to do? More importantly, when will I be clear to work? My shoulder is healed up well enough, and I'm ready."

"The investigation into your last assignment hasn't been closed. You won't be back in fugitive apprehension until the assessment is complete."

Joanna gripped the edges of the chair. "I'm on desk?"

Don smiled slightly. "Not quite that bad. You're going undercover for WITSEC."

"Witness security?" she echoed faintly. "But I don't do witness protection. I chase bad guys, remember?"

Joanna lived for the chase. Always on the move, she'd taken down some of the worst of the worst. WITSEC, in her opinion, was nothing more than glorified babysitting. It was too slow and didn't have nearly the excitement hunting down a fugitive offered.

"No way, I—"

"Listen, I know what you think of witness protection, but you go undercover to protect Ben Callahan or your backside is warming one of those chairs out there until the investigation into your last assignment is complete."

"This sucks. I made one mistake, one small error in judgment—"

"You nearly got yourself killed and almost lost out on the apprehension of a dangerous suspect in the process. You pushed too hard, put yourself and the case at risk, and it's not the first time. You need to dial things down a notch. Just for a while."

"You don't get the guys we're after by backing off."

"I know, and you're one of the best we've got. But right now, you need to do this. Believe me, it took some wrangling for me to even get you this assignment, and that's only because WITSEC is stretched to capacity. They need you."

Suddenly it became clear to her why she'd been brought into this conversation.

"The cowboy? I thought he'd refused any protection," she said.

"He did. And you seem to agree that a stranger would stick out like a sore thumb, but I think you could fit right in. He runs a roadhouse on his family ranch near Midland, and it just so happens they're looking for help."

"You've got to be kidding."

He didn't so much as crack a smile.

Joanna took a deep breath, settling back in the chair,

trying to accept her fate. Undercover might not be too bad. At least it was out of the office, in the field, and if this is what it took to get the shrinks and administrators off her back, then fine.

"How long?"

"Three weeks. Keep him safe, let us know if there's anything else going on—if you think he's hiding something, if there's a threat he's not telling us about, some other reason he would refuse protection, anything. He can't find out who you are—this is our only shot. If he makes you, we could lose him altogether. Don't downplay this, Jo. And if things get messy, you call for backup—not like the last time."

"Of course," she said, crossing her arms. "But for the record, I did call for backup. It's in the report. It's not my fault they took forever to show up and I had to try to handle things myself."

"Got it. But what happens next in your career rests on making this assignment work. I don't want to lose you, so, like I said, make it work."

Joanna could only nod. She was a professional, and an assignment was an assignment, but God help her, the next three weeks couldn't pass quickly enough.

On her last case, she'd made a mistake. She'd decided not to wait for backup during a takedown—there wasn't time, in her assessment, if they didn't want a serial rapist to get away—and she'd taken a bullet for her trouble.

It was the only time she'd ever been shot, and it had almost been the last time. Missed a major coronary artery by an inch. She would have bled out so quickly she wouldn't even have known what happened. The guy had been apprehended a little later, but it hadn't been by her. That stung almost more than the gunshot.

Now, there was penance to be paid, and hers was babysitting Ben Callahan.

1

BEN CALLAHAN PAUSED IN THE doorway of the Lucky Break, the bar that he'd inherited from his grandfather, trying to figure out what was different. Scanning his surroundings, his senses honed by nearly eleven years as a navy SEAL, his gaze finally landed on the source of his curiosity.

Her.

A good deal of smooth, shapely feminine thigh was exposed by the short denim skirt that also showed off a spectacular bottom line. He wasn't the only one who noticed. Men filing in for the lunch hour bestowed appreciative glances on the new waitress as she walked from table to table taking orders.

Dark-brown hair was caught in a loose ponytail that swished around her shoulder blades as she moved. The movement drew his attention to her strong, slim shoulders, tight waistline and long, graceful neck.

As she turned, he saw she wasn't big on top, but she sure made the most of what she had. *A tall drink of water,* was the phrase his mother often used; it came to mind as he watched his new waitress.

Charlie, his best friend and second in command at the bar, had been in charge of hiring while Ben was out of town talking to the Feds. He didn't want to be away any longer than he needed to, given the circumstances, but now he could stick close to home.

Fortunately, Charlie had been lucky with finding a new waitress for them. Interviewing new help wasn't a job Ben relished, even as owner of the place, mostly because his mother was too likely to send in the daughters of her friends, who were better candidates for marriage than waitressing. Then there were former girlfriends who came around since he'd been back, some of them still single, others divorced.

That was the problem with returning to the town where you grew up. He still wasn't completely used to it. It had only been a year, and leaving military life behind hadn't been an easy choice.

Family, legacy and land often went together in Texas. Those ties meant something—it was a lesson he'd learned in the SEALs, where connections to your team meant everything. They meant your life. Connections to your family worked the same way, that was how Ben saw it, anyhow. He had served his country and now he served his family.

As well as copious amounts of beer to the locals.

When his grandfather had died, Ben hadn't been home in over two years. He couldn't change that, but he could do his granddad proud now.

Ben was slowly getting used to civilian life and he enjoyed it, for the most part. He'd moved into the old house behind the bar, and he had picked back up with rodeo, mostly bullriding and some roping. He was used to regular adrenaline highs, and rodeo satisfied that urge as well as possibly garnering championships for his parents' ranch.

The last show he had been in had provided a little more excitement than he'd been looking for, though, when he'd seen a murder. One of the judges from the rodeo was shot, execution style. Ben had been in the wrong place at the right time, witnessing the whole thing—though he hadn't been able to stop it.

It turned out it wasn't a crime of opportunity, but had been connected to organized crime's attempts to control large rodeo purses by drugging animals and by pressuring the judges. The man they'd killed had been one of the judges who had refused to play along. His three kids were now left without a father.

The killer was now in San Antonio, and Ben's testimony was going to put him away. Or, as the U.S. Attorney's office would have it, Ben's testimony would give them the leverage to make a deal that would lead to the bigger players the killer worked for. The FBI was involved, and the U.S. Marshals, and who knew who else? That split second had turned Ben's life upside down.

He knew from his military experience that a smaller evil was often the price of stopping a larger one. It was how the world worked, but he didn't have to like it.

He was also perfectly aware that, because the deal or the conviction rested on his testimony, he was in a certain degree of danger right now.

So he'd canceled his late-summer rodeo appearances for this year, claiming he needed to be home to run the business. The government had offered him protection, which meant living at a safe house until the trial, but that wouldn't help his family or friends. They'd even offered him Witness Protection, but he wasn't about to leave the life to which he had just returned.

Besides, SEALs didn't run.

The trial was in three weeks, the Justice Department had done a good job of keeping his identity out of circulation; they'd squelched any news stories about the incident, so Ben hoped they would get to the end of this without trouble. So far, so good.

"Welcome back, boss," Charlie said, closing the space between them as he walked out of the kitchen, spotting Ben standing by the door.

Ben smiled and clasped his friend's hand tightly.

"Good to see the place still standing, Charlie."

"It was a lonely four days. We did okay. Good to have you back, though."

"Thanks," Ben said, and looked at the new waitress again.

This time, she noticed him too. Looking at him with big, dark-brown eyes, she smiled slightly and then turned back to her customer. "New girl?"

"Yeah. She's doing a great job, so far, though it's only day two."

"Don't recognize her from around here," Ben said neutrally, but his mind was on immediate alert.

Anyone new was a question mark. Normally Ben wouldn't question a stranger showing up for a job, but right now, things were a little touchier than usual.

"She broke up with her boyfriend, came down from El Paso looking for a job and a place to stay. Seems capable enough, and she sure is nice to look at," Charlie said with a grin, his eyes noting some of the same attributes that Ben had been admiring. "Um, I rented her the apartment upstairs, too. Figured, what the heck? At least we know she won't be late for work."

Ben's frown was his response to that news. Of course, Charlie didn't know about Ben's situation. Ben didn't want anyone to worry when there might not be anything to worry about.

"I had to do it, Ben," Charlie said, reading his expression. "When I came in yesterday, she was sleeping in her car in the parking lot. I couldn't let her stay there until she had enough paychecks to get a place. Besides, she agreed to work extra shifts in exchange for no rent."

"You check references, get her background?" Ben asked casually, walking toward the kitchen.

"Do I look like an idiot?" Charlie asked.

"Nope, but I know you and beautiful women, my friend," Ben said with a smile. "She could be the worst waitress on the planet or a convicted felon, but looking like that..."

"Don't worry, I checked her out. Joanna Wallace. Nothing significant, the usual history of dead-end retail and restaurant jobs. No convictions, clean driver's license. Nice enough. Seems to have made a few bad choices about the men she takes up with, though she didn't share too many details."

Ben nodded, glancing through a stack of mail he picked up from the counter. It was easy enough to create a history, set up references, but he was also being paranoid. He'd put a sign out front and someone had come by to apply for the job. Why not her?

Besides, if the mob wanted to take him out, Ben doubted they would send someone like that, he mused. Still, he'd check her out through his own sources as soon as he could.

"Thanks, Charlie. I appreciate you taking that task off my shoulders," Ben said.

"No problem. Lisa likes her, too, if that helps. I let her interview her as well before we made a final decision."

Ben nodded. "That was smart."

Lisa was his one full-time waitress, but her husband had recently left her with their two kids. While she took extra shifts, they needed someone else to cover gaps and help out during the busiest times. Lisa was worth her weight in gold, and it was important that she could work with whomever they hired.

"I'm missing a leg, not a brain," his friend reprised jokingly, as he often did about the limb he was missing after repeated tours in Iraq. The last tour had seen his leg blown off in a roadside explosion. Yet Charlie never complained, more often using humor to make others comfortable.

"I didn't balance the books this week. You know I suck at math, so I thought I'd leave that to you," Charlie added.

"I knew I should have stayed away a few more days," Ben said with a rueful shake of his head, making both of them laugh as Charlie returned to the grill.

Ben planned to hire a bookkeeper one of these days. For now, he was learning something new every day about running the business, and knowing the financials was as important as anything else. So, he did the books, the ordering, and everything else that came with running a roadhouse, and he was slowly learning the tricks of the trade. He'd hung out here all the time as a kid, helping his grandfather, and then as a teen, meeting here with his friends. The Lucky Break was a large part of his life, though he needed to upgrade some things. He now also appreciated all of the work it took to run a successful establishment.

It was a challenge he could dig into, focus on, and he owed his grandfather the best job he could do. To Ben's amazement, as the months passed, he enjoyed it more and more. There was always something to keep him busy, and when he wasn't doing something here, he was fixing up the house, working at his parents' ranch down the road, or practicing for the next rodeo.

While he'd loved being a SEAL, real life definitely had its attractions, he thought as he walked out from the kitchen to the bar. Washing his hands, his gaze landed on the new waitress again.

Lisa, also working the lunch shift, winked at him and waved. Ben nodded back, slipping behind the bar to pitch in with the increasing lunch crowd.

Joanna approached the bar with an order. Close up, she was even more stunning. He almost wouldn't have blamed Charlie if he had hired her for her looks.

"Two drafts and one cola," she said, her brown eyes meeting his as she shot her hand over the bar in greeting. "Hi, I'm Joanna. Lisa tells me you're the boss."

He nodded, his eyes drifting to her lips. She wore no lipstick, just some gloss, and her skin was also unadorned, no cosmetics marring her clear, tanned complexion.

"Ben, Ben Callahan," he offered calmly enough, though her touch and her eyes had almost turned him hard with immediate lust, right here behind his bar. She had a strong grip for a woman, those long, slim fingers closing around his, but her skin was like satin.

Ben cleared his throat, letting go of her hand and

turning to pull down some glasses for the beer and the soda, loading them up on a tray and handing them back to her. He wasn't used to losing control, certainly not from one touch.

"Thanks," she said, starting to turn away.

"Joanna," he said, stopping her, his mind clearing.

"Yes?"

"Make some time to talk for a few minutes after your shift? Maybe catch a bite? I like to touch base with new employees, you understand," he said.

She nodded, seeming unfazed. "Sure, no problem."

Watching her walk away, the little alarm in his brain just wouldn't settle down. He couldn't quite figure out why, but there was something about her that didn't scream down-on-her-luck. She also didn't seem like a woman to take up with the wrong kind of guy. Self-confidence and intelligence practically crackled in the air around her as she moved.

She exuded an earthy sexuality that had likely brought more than one man to his knees. The vision of what he'd like to do on his knees before Joanna Wallace made him shake his head, and he got back to work, turning to greet and take the lunch orders from a couple of local ranch hands who pulled up to the bar.

He supposed his physical reaction to a beautiful woman wasn't out of the usual. Ben hadn't been with anyone in a while. Life had been too crazy.

He'd had a one-nighter on his last military leave, and that was well over a year ago. Since then, things had just not lined up in the right way. Not that he hadn't had some offers since he'd come home, but he didn't want to make things more complicated in his own backyard.

And truthfully, none of the women he'd met had inspired him that way.

Joanna Wallace definitely inspired him. Still, lust was mingling with caution in a very uncomfortable way.

As he conducted his work at the bar, he watched her interact with a table of customers who seemed captivated by her. She joked with them, smiling broadly, her laugh rising over the din of the room. Her eyes met his across the space again, as if she'd felt him watching her. She was aware of him, too.

Interesting.

Her posture, the slight apprehension in the way she held her shoulders when she looked at him, told him what he wanted to know. Part of it, anyway. She was hiding something, and by the end of the afternoon, he intended to know what it was.

JOANNA DIDN'T REMEMBER ever being so nervous that her palms were as sweaty as they were when she walked into the employee lounge to meet Ben Callahan.

She'd had to fight her instinct to cover up the generous amount of skin exposed by the halter top she was wearing. Definitely not her usual style. Lacey, her brother Jarod's wife, had insisted it was perfect for a job at a roadhouse. In truth, Joanna had felt pretty comfortable in the get-up until Ben Callahan had looked at her. Then she had been distinctly uncomfortable in a couple of different ways.

Getting by Charlie and Lisa had been easy, but when Ben looked at her, she had the feeling he knew right away that she wasn't who she said she was. Not a waitress, not Joanna Wallace. She half expected him to call her out on it right then and there, but her background cover was solid, even if they checked.

Now she was going to meet with him privately, and she had to convince him she was the real deal. Tom's words about her career hanging on her success rang in her head and as she closed the door, walked toward the thick wooden table where he sat with two of the cheeseburger specials that she'd been serving all during lunch. Her stomach growled. She was hungry. Waitressing, something she hadn't done since college, was hard physical work.

"Hi, hope you don't mind a burger," Ben said congenially, though his eyes were telling her a different story. He wasn't sure of her yet, and he was suspicious.

That was good. Of course, given his military background, she assumed he would be cautious. He knew the score, knew that what he'd seen put him in a certain amount of danger. He'd be particularly careful about anyone he didn't know. She'd expected that.

"This is great, thanks," she said with a smile and took the chair across from him.

"Eat, then we can talk," he said, grabbing his own sandwich.

She had no argument with that.

Polishing off his burger, he sat back and waited for her. She didn't rush, and also sat back with a contented sigh when she finished.

"I don't know what Charlie does to these burgers, but he deserves some kind of medal," she said to break the ice.

"He does have talent at the grill," Callahan agreed, and didn't break eye contact as the tone shifted between them. "So, tell me a little about yourself. I know Charlie crossed the t's and dotted the i's, but I like to know who's working for me."

She shrugged. "What do you want to know?"

"You're clearly from Texas, but not local. Where'd you grow up?"

"Just outside Corpus Christi, though I've lived in San Diego for the last eight years. Came back to El Paso with my boyfriend, Lenny. It didn't work out."

The best lies were couched in as much truth as possible, and while she had been living in San Diego when she was shot, and she did have a former boyfriend named Lenny, everything else was pure fiction. She waited for him to respond.

Taking another sip of her drink, her throat was suddenly dry for no reason other than he was one of the best-looking men she'd ever seen. Six-foot-plus of lean, incredible Texas male.

She had been raised by two strong men, her dad and her older brother, Jarod, who were both Texas Rangers and were also all the family she'd ever known after her mom had taken off when Joanna was seven. For this reason, she had always been very comfortable around men.

She worked with lots of very good-looking men in her job—ones easily as good-looking as Ben Callahan—but they were marshals, and she never thought of them romantically. Even back in high school, she'd found the boys easier to get along with, and had had more male than female friends.

For that reason, Joanna dated very rarely. She'd been halfway through college before she'd lost her virginity, and even that was with a guy she considered more of a friend than a lover. He was an Assistant District Attorney in Houston now, married, with four kids.

None of that was ever part of Joanna's plan. She was all about the job, just like her brother and her father.

Except that Jarod was married now, and even her father had met someone.

That was nice. She was happy for them, and she loved her sister-in-law Lacey. But she wasn't about to follow suit.

For all these reasons, it was mortifying that her breath caught when Ben Callahan leaned in closer over the table. She snapped her mouth shut, realizing she had actually licked her lip.

Make it work for you, you're supposed to be nervous. Play the part.

He had to believe she was just a waitress, a girl down on her luck who'd made some bad choices and who needed the job. If she couldn't pull that off, her supervisors would think she had really lost her touch.

A dark-blond lock fell forward on his forehead, and he pushed it back, every muscle in his arm showing off in the process. She could almost make out the movement of his abs under the white T-shirt he wore.

She'd memorized his file, of course, though none of the pictures there did him justice. He'd been out of the SEALs for less than a year, retired with an honorable discharge. She wondered what had happened. In her experience, those guys never left until they were forced to. Whatever it was, he still stayed in fighting form.

She dropped her eyes to his hands where they rested on the table. It crossed her mind that she could have gotten laid sometime in the last four or five weeks.

Joanna liked sex, but had always thought of it more

like a sport, something to do that scratched an itch more than anything else, though there hadn't been much chance for that recently. In fact, it had been the last thing on her mind until about two minutes ago. Ben Callahan was sex personified, and her previously dormant hormones were picking a hell of a time to wake up.

He was talking to her, and she was so busy processing her lust that she wasn't paying attention to what he was saying, yanking herself back to the present moment.

"Charlie said you were sleeping in your car, and he rented you the room upstairs?"

"Yeah, he's a great guy," she said.

"So there's no family to help out, no other place you could go?"

She shifted in her seat. She had to give him something he would believe.

"Well, I do have a brother, but to be honest, he's not too interested in having me around. I'm also trying to stay off the radar. I don't want Lenny trying to find me. Not that he would, but you know, it can't hurt to be careful."

"Why?" His tone lowered, and his eyes narrowed slightly.

"Well, I thought I was giving him money to get his truck fixed and it turns out it was for drug deals. I swear, I had no idea," she said quickly, appearing as desperate as she could. "I had no idea he was buying stuff and reselling it until he got really angry when he came up short, got in some trouble, and I refused to help."

"And?"

"Well, he got a bit rough, and I knew I was in trouble if I stayed, so I sort of stole his truck to get out of there. He owed me, you know? I had given him hundreds of dollars."

"And you had no idea he was into drugs?"

"Not really. He had used a few times, but that's a long way from dealing. And I don't have anything to do with that stuff," she said convincingly. "I thought he was a nice guy, but I thought wrong."

He watched her carefully for a few minutes, and she closed her hands into fists on the table top, a not completely false show of tension.

"So where's the truck?"

"I traded it for my car at a used car place—you know, roadside, the guy didn't ask many questions since the truck was worth more than the car I got. I paid him extra not to tell anyone. Then I was out of funds and I was sick of living in my car, so I looked for a job."

She saw Callahan's spine straighten. "I see. So you're afraid this guy will come after you? Lenny?"

"He probably won't, but if he does, he'd never think that I would stay here," she said, smiling slightly, as if pleased with herself. "He'll think I went back to San Diego."

Ben didn't smile back.

"But he might. I don't appreciate trouble like this being brought to my door and not being told about it. You weren't exactly straight with Charlie."

She frowned and leaned in, too, getting closer. His pupils dilated slightly, and from that, and how he had looked at her earlier, she knew he was attracted to her. That gave her some leverage.

"I know, I'm so sorry," she said, licking her lip again

in a gesture of nervousness. "But I had to get away, and I did what I had to do. I just want to get back to my life. I honestly don't think Lenny will come after me. He's not that ambitious. I'm sure he's found someone new to sponge off by now."

There was no Lenny, of course, so she was one-hundred-percent sure that no one would be showing up here after her.

Ben considered, and then nodded slowly. "He didn't report you for stealing his truck?"

She snorted. "He would have to risk me telling them about the drugs."

"That's true," he said, nodding. "Well, I'm glad you got out. And you're doing a good job here, so I have no problem with you staying on. But if he does show up, or if there's any kind of trouble—"

"I'll leave," she finished for him.

"No. You'll tell one of us—me or Charlie—directly."

He really was a white knight, she thought. It made being here for him better, and lying to him harder.

"Oh, okay. I'll do that," she promised.

"Good. Anything else I should know?"

"I'm a really good waitress. I'll work hard, keep my hands out of the till. I never stole a dime until taking that truck, so you don't have to worry. I just need to get back on my feet," she said, hoping she'd hit the sweet spot between being someone he would want to help, who'd had trouble but who wasn't going to *be* trouble.

Ben nodded and sat back. "What about your brother?"

"He wrote me off years ago. Never really cared much about what happened to me after our parents were gone."

Sorry, Jarod, she offered the mental mea culpa to her brother, who was the best of the best. She loved him madly, and he'd always been there for her and always would be, but she knew plenty of people whose families weren't. Thinking of her mom, Joanna never failed to be surprised at how easy it was for some people to walk away from the ones they were supposed to love most.

"That's tough. Well, the job is yours as long as you want it."

She smiled in relief. He'd bought it. She was in.

"Thanks. I really appreciate that. And the trade on rent. I really didn't want to find a motel, and the nearest one is ten miles down, from what Charlie said," she added. "And you know, with gas prices so high…"

"It's good that someone's using the apartment. Anything you need up there? It didn't come with much."

"I don't need much. Though I do have to find a discount store to buy a few fans. It's hot at night," she said, absently moving a loose strand of hair from her cheek.

He followed the movement closely, and she was surprised to feel an answering sizzle of interest in her own bloodstream.

"I may have an extra one or two at my house. I can bring them up tonight."

"No need, I—"

"No problem. Supposed to be over one hundred tomorrow. No point in being uncomfortable up there. It's a small space as it is."

"Thanks," she said with a smile. "Is that all?"

"Yeah, for now. Thanks," he said, standing, so she did too.

She was nearly his height, but he still was a few

inches taller than her five-eleven and considerably more massive.

Still, she'd taken down guys his size and couldn't help thinking about what it would be like to wrestle with Ben Callahan.

Before she gave anything away, she shelved that thought and turned toward the door, leaving without another word.

Ben Callahan was smart and perceptive. She had her work cut out for her, Joanna knew, walking through the kitchen and back up the stairs to her small apartment. She had to pull this off; her career and his life, potentially, counted on it.

No pressure at all.

2

THE NEXT AFTERNOON, BEN watched Joanna from the kitchen door, following the perfect shape of her ass in those jeans as she worked the lunch crowd as though she'd been doing it for years.

He stopped gawking to go help at the bar, serving up beers and getting into the flow and rhythm of the lunch hour, which didn't leave time to think about much else. Except when he handed a tray of drinks and sandwiches to Joanna who took them with a polite, businesslike smile and turned away.

His thoughts were not as businesslike every time he thought about those long, long legs.

She'd checked out, though. He'd run his own background check, run her car, called a few people, and nothing seemed out of place. So, for now, he was just enjoying the view, he thought with a smile as he watched her walk away.

He hadn't kept his promise about bringing the fans up to her the night before, and she hadn't said a word about it. He knew the apartment was hotter than a sauna in mid-summer, but she didn't complain or make demands.

Truth was, his fans weren't going to help much, and so he'd driven into Midland the evening before to buy an air-conditioning unit for the space, and had gotten back too late to bring it up to her. He planned to install it today.

"You have the look of a starving man, bucko," Charlie said with a laugh, sidling up beside him. "And Joanna looks like dinner."

"You're imagining things, Charlie."

"No, I'm not. Been a while since you hooked up with anyone. Do you some good," Charlie, always the practical one, said. "She looks like she could give you a good—"

"Don't," Ben said, cutting his friend off a little more harshly than he meant to, and then slapped his buddy's shoulder to ease the words. "I need a waitress more than I need to get laid," Ben said, turning away.

"Says you," Charlie said, grabbing a bucket of glasses to carry out back.

Ben had been in a less than cheerful mood recently. He couldn't wait for this damned trial to be over with so he could return to his life. The noise in the bar softened as the lunch crowd started thinning, as workers from the local ranches and other businesses headed to their jobs.

Joanna returned to the bar, took a seat, a thin shine of perspiration on her forehead as she smiled at him. He liked her dark, espresso-brown eyes. She was friendly with the customers, but didn't flirt—with him, either, though there was chemistry between them—no doubt about that. There was a seriousness about her that suggested depth, and he suddenly wanted to know what books she read, what movies she liked. In the next second, he pulled those thoughts out by the root. This wasn't a good time, and fooling around with the help was never a good idea.

Ben pushed a glass with ice and a soda across the bar at her and pretended not to notice the slim muscles in her arms, or the delicate arch of her throat as she drank it.

"Can I get you some lunch?" he asked.

"In a little while. I have to help Lisa finish cleaning up, but thanks for the drink. Hot today, even in here, with the AC."

"Yeah, speaking of that, I'm sorry I didn't bring the fans up last night, but I went into the city and got an AC unit instead. I can put that in today. It should help a lot. Fans would just push the hot air around."

She looked sincerely surprised, like someone who didn't expect people to do nice things for her.

"Hey, hot as it is, it's a million times better than my car," she joked with a grin.

"It's no problem. I should have done it a while ago. If you want, I can go up and put it in while you're helping Lisa, and—"

"No, really, it's fine if you want to just wait until later," she said quickly.

He paused. There it was again, that itchy feeling that something was off.

"I mean, I'm kind of a slob. I don't want you walking in when I'd left stuff all over the floor, you know, laundry and that kind of thing," she said with a self-effacing grin.

He relaxed again. "Sure, no problem. Tonight's fine," he agreed.

Ben supposed that made sense. It was her space for as long as she was renting, and it wasn't unreasonable not to want a stranger pawing through her things, not that he would. Considering the relationship she was in before now, he couldn't blame her for being apprehensive.

"Thanks for the drink. I'm going to go help Lisa," she said, slipping from the chair and walking back to the kitchen.

Ben put the glass he had been polishing for the past ten minutes back on the shelf behind the bar and closed his eyes, taking a breath and trying to focus. He was rarely this scattered, but Joanna was very distracting.

Maybe Charlie was right. Maybe he should do something about that. It wasn't good policy to sleep with the help, and she was bouncing off a bad relationship—not the best situation for either of them—but his mind kept traveling back to the same idea.

And he kept pushing it aside. There were plenty of women around to sleep with, if that's what he wanted, but he needed Joanna on the job.

That was a shame, he thought, as she came back out from the kitchen carrying a tray of freshly filled ketchup bottles, the motion of it deepening the slight cleavage at the edge of her tank top.

A real shame.

JOANNA DUSTED HER HANDS OFF ON her jeans, feeling better as she made her way around the small, basic apartment where dust had collected everywhere. She hadn't had much time to clean or set the place up yet, and so she worked off some excess energy doing so now.

Changing into her comfortable jeans and a loose white T-shirt was nirvana, shucking the boots for a pair of well-broken-in sandals. Her job took her everywhere, but having her comfortable clothes with her was how she felt at home wherever she was, and this was no different.

After two hours of cleaning, the place sparkled. Callahan wasn't kidding when he said it was small. One main room had a sofa, a small easy chair and a television. Off the hallway that led to the back, there was a galley kitchen with a mini fridge but no stove.

There was a hotplate and an old-fashioned metal coffeepot on the counter, but she supposed a stove wasn't necessary when they had a whole restaurant downstairs. Down at the very end of the hall was a bedroom with a futon-like bed and a table, next to it was a tiny, utilitarian bathroom.

Everything was painted a monotone beige, not that it mattered to her at the moment. Her apartment in San Diego had been painted in rich, nourishing colors that were a warm welcome when she came home after a long time on the job. Now, she was between living spaces. During her recovery and transfer, she had lived with her brother and Lacey. She wasn't sure where she wanted to land permanently yet, though she thought being back in Texas might not be all bad. Spending time with her family again had been nice.

When she had first walked in to the apartment, the windows were closed and the heat was stagnant and suffocating. Now, it was early evening and with every window open—thank goodness the screens were intact—there was a nice breeze coming in. It was still warm, but pleasant enough. She relaxed for a few minutes, looking out over the pastures and hills that sprawled beyond the parking lot of the roadhouse. It was probably going to rain tonight. She could smell it on the air.

Crickets were singing down below. After her mom had taken off, Joanna had had nightmares for months, and she had often had fears of someone being outside her bedroom window in the small, one-floor ranch home that they lived in. It was irrational, but she would wake up terrified and ask her dad to check outside her room several times each night.

So her father had shown her one night how if she listened for the crickets, they would let her know if anyone was really there. He went outside and walked up to her bedroom window several times, and each time, sure enough, the crickets went silent.

Crickets still made her feel safe, content, to this day.

The place was more than adequate for her needs, and it allowed her to be right on top of Callahan a good part of the time. She stopped in the middle of grabbing a beer from the mini-fridge, thinking about all the different ways she'd like to be on top of Ben Callahan.

Being closer to Callahan, however she managed it, would be a good thing—or potentially a bad one—if she let things go too far. There was a definite spark there. She knew he wanted her—and in some ways, she'd be stupid not to capitalize on that attraction to keep a closer eye on him.

However, there were strict rules governing the relationship between marshals and the people they protected, and non-fraternization was one of them.

However, Callahan wasn't a part of the WITSEC program, so those rules *technically* didn't apply, though sharing his bed could be a problem in a number of professional and ethical ways.

Not that anyone would have to find out.

The problem was…well, she wasn't exactly sure what the problem was, she thought, slouching back in the chair by the window. It wasn't as if she was going to fall in love with him or something. If it got the job done and took the edge off, why not?

But she couldn't talk herself into it.

While no doubt it would be entertaining, Joanna found the idea of sleeping with someone as part of her job distasteful. Flirting a little, or even going on a date, was acceptable. If it helped her to keep him safe, she was okay with that.

Luckily, her phone ringing on the counter discouraged any further fantasizing. She grabbed it, looking at the screen and seeing her brother Jarod's name pop up.

"Hi, Jarod. What's up? Everything okay?"

"Everything's great. How's it going?"

Her brother cared about her, but he never checked up on her. He absolutely never called her when she was on assignment. Knowing what undercover work was like, he wouldn't want to do anything to throw her out of her mindset.

"Lacey pestering you to call and see how I am?" she asked, smiling as she realized why her brother was making an exception to the rule.

"How'd you guess? Sorry about this, but she's been worrying about you all day. She wouldn't have slept a wink unless I spoke with you."

"Tell her thanks, and it all went great. Got the job, and even scored an apartment above the bar."

"Excellent for surveillance."

"Exactly."

"How's your new employer?"

She shrugged, moving out of the kitchen to go sit on the sofa by the window. "Okay. What you would expect, I guess."

Both of them knew better than to share anything too specific on the phone. She'd have to keep this short, as nice as it was to talk to her brother.

"By the way, Lacey wants me to let you know there's a 'cute condo' here in San Antonio that her friend is selling, if you are interested in seeing it when you get back," Jarod related, obviously being pushed to do so.

"Tell her maybe I'll look at it," she said, and then her phone beeped and she saw her boss's name pop up. "Jarod, gotta go—Don is on the other line."

"Take care of yourself, jelly bean," Jarod said affectionately, making her smile again by using the nickname he always called her.

"You, too," she said, hanging up, and answering the other call.

"Wyatt," she answered, as she always did for work.

"You in?" Don asked in a no-nonsense tone as she stood and paced the small room.

"Yeah, no problem."

"Good. You're not still sleeping in your car, are you?"

"No," she said, stifling a grin. Don was her boss, but he was also a friend who sometimes acted like a second big brother. Although he never cut her any slack when it came to work, and she wouldn't expect him to. "Callahan had a room free up over the bar, so I took it."

"Good work. Anything going on?"

"Nope. Pretty dull."

"Don't sound so disappointed. You could use some dull."

"Then I'll be back chasing bad guys in a few weeks?" she asked hopefully.

"We'll see. A few things are still to be untangled about your part in that last case. And you could use more recovery time before you're back out there."

"Don, seriously, I'm—"

"Just go with it, Jo," he interrupted, reminding her that chafing at the restrictions wouldn't help. "This is an easy assignment, but an important one."

"Just keep an eye on him, and keep a low profile—or try to. I know it's not your strength," he said dryly.

"Fine. If you could send me dossiers on a couple people he has working here, that would help."

She gave him Charlie's and Lisa's names. She would feel better once she knew more about the people around Callahan. You never really knew who the enemy was in these cases.

"Will do. You'll get them electronically. Check in when you can. We don't have any backup out there for you in the immediate vicinity except for local law enforcement, so if you see trouble, let us know ASAP. Don't try to handle it yourself. Do you hear that, Jo?"

Hearing a squeak in the boards outside her door, she turned, and changed her tone to a whisper.

"Same as I've heard it the twenty other times you said it," she responded smartly. "Gotta go. I'll be in touch," she said, hanging up and walking closer to the door, listening.

She didn't know if she had just imagined the noise or not.

It could just be the musicians setting up downstairs. Thursdays, Fridays and Saturdays the roadhouse had live bands playing, and she'd seen the guys drive in and unpack their gear while she was on the phone.

Her apartment would not be quiet until well past midnight tonight, or for the next few nights, but if the music was good, maybe she'd go downstairs and enjoy it.

A thudding sound, and then a hard, loud knock had her stepping back in surprise, bumping into the table and knocking over the lamp on the small table by the door, her heart hammering. The lamp didn't break, and she picked it back up, settling it on the table.

"Joanna?" she heard Callahan's voice on the other side. "What was that? Are you okay?"

She grimaced, standing and setting her phone on the table before she opened the door to find him standing there, a boxed air conditioner at his feet.

"Everything okay in there?" he asked, peering past.

"Fine. I just upset the lamp on my way to the door," she said, her pulse calming somewhat as she looked back down at the AC unit.

"Here's the air conditioner. I can get it installed in just a few minutes. Where do you want it?"

Joanna watched appreciatively as he bent to pick up the appliance, which wasn't small. She enjoyed watching the strong play of muscles in his shoulders and back as he did so.

Swallowing hard, she hoped her warm cheeks didn't give her away as he met her eyes again.

"So, where do you want it?"

"I'm fine, actually. The place is great with all the windows open."

He shook his head doubtfully. "Supposed to get up over one hundred again tomorrow."

"You didn't need to go to so much trouble."

She was screwing this up, she knew, and chastised herself for arguing with him. Any form of connection she could forge with Callahan would help her do her job, so why was she rebuffing him? Something about him just made her…itchy.

"Okay, if you say so," he said, shrugging muscular shoulders as if the air conditioner didn't weigh a thing.

He turned away, and she closed her eyes, blowing out a breath and sucking up her natural self-reliance. Joanna Wyatt, the U.S. Marshal, didn't need a guy to take care of her or worry about her, but Joanna Wallace, the waitress without a penny to her name, would not refuse this kindness. And it was hot in the apartment, even with the windows open.

"Wait," she said, stepping out onto the small, square landing in front of the door and putting a hand on his back to stop his progress.

They both stilled, and she paused a moment before taking her hand away. He turned, his eyes seeming a little darker, a little hotter.

"Yes?"

"Listen, thanks. It would probably make nights more comfortable. I just didn't want you doing me any special favors."

"It's just an air-conditioner."

She nodded. Callahan was a stand-up guy. A nice guy.

She was being ridiculous. This was about her and her hormones, not about him.

"Uh, this is getting heavy," he said, interrupting her train of thought. "I thought the bedroom might be the best idea?"

Her heart rate skyrocketed. "What?"

"It will keep it cool at night. For sleeping," he said, not seeming to notice her reaction.

"Oh, right, that makes sense," she agreed, stepping back into the apartment and holding the door open for him.

"Bedroom it is," he said, and walked past her and then back to the bedroom.

Holding her breath and praying he would leave before she gave in to her baser instincts, she followed him into the small bedroom, ignoring every warning bell that was ringing in her head.

Joanna turned out of the room and went back to the kitchen, pacing, as she listened to Callahan in her bedroom wrestling the air conditioner into the small window. When she heard profuse cursing, she gave in and went to see if she could help. Surely she was not so pathetic as not to be able to stand in a room with the man, was she?

"Everything okay?" she asked from the doorway. "Do you need help?" Was that her voice sounding a pitch higher and slightly breathless?

"As much as it dents my masculine ego to admit it, I could use a hand with this window," he said with a short laugh. "The sash cord seems to be broken, and I nearly got my hand caught in there on the last try," he said. He was squatting on the floor in the small space between the bed and the window, wearing a chagrined smile.

She nodded, crawling over the bed, the only way to get to the other side of the air conditioner without crawling over *him*.

She wasn't trying to be enticing, but as she crawled on all fours over the fresh linens that Lisa had brought up, she saw a muscle tick in his jaw as he watched her.

It made her want to lick the spot.

He might let her, too. She'd been around enough men to sense that particular sort of tension in their bodies, that look that said they wanted to get naked as soon as possible.

She was here in a small, overly warm bedroom with a sexy hunk of a guy who she was pretty sure could make her sleep well tonight. Or not sleep at all.

A noise from below, the strong strum of a guitar chord made her jump, and she looked up, seeing him smile.

"Forgot the band was warming up."

"They any good?" she asked, making small talk as she swung her legs over and squatted down on the opposite side of the AC unit, pinched between the wall and the bed's frame.

"They're good. One of the more popular bands around here. Helps the draw on Thursdays," he said, and her hand brushed his forearm as they wrangled the unit into position.

The idea of being wrapped in Callahan's powerful arms, keeping her warm all night long, flooded her mind. She had sexual fantasies about guys—who didn't? But she never thought about them holding her through the night as she slept. She'd never been one for romance novels or lovey-dovey fantasizing. Still, tripping over her thirtieth year a few months before, and thinking about that bullet drifting an inch in the other direction made her wonder about what she might have been missing in her life. Spending time with her brother and Lacey had only driven that home for her, but at the end of the day, Joanna was the job. She loved it, and she didn't know anything else. She certainly wouldn't give it all up for a man.

Ben seemed absolutely clueless about her inner conflict as he managed to line up the unit with the window frame once more.

"If you can hold the window up while I get this positioned, that would be great," he directed, distracting her yet again with how the T-shirt he wore clung to his skin in the hot room.

"Sure," she said casually and pushed the window up, holding it higher than necessary so that he had room to maneuver.

Within a few minutes, he had the air conditioner fitted tightly into the window, and it was ready to go. As Joanna let the window down, he leaned over to plug it in, and then set it so that cool air immediately started pulsing out of the appliance.

It felt great, Joanna had to admit, and pushed her hair back from where it clung to her cheek. When she looked down, she caught him staring up from the floor, his attention clearly caught by the way her nipples were at full attention from the cold air blasting on her.

He turned away, fussing with something.

"It's a small room. Probably can set this on low," he said, more to himself than to her, and Joanna murmured something just as unintelligible.

She wasn't even aware of what she said, more to herself than to him; she'd rarely felt chemistry like this, not this fast anyway.

Thinking he was going to turn around to walk out, she moved in that direction as well, but he leaned down to get some packing plastic that had dropped on the floor.

Legs tangled, arms flailed, and a second later, Joanna was sprawled on the firm mattress with Callahan spread over the top of her.

The cool air from the AC on her bare feet made her shiver—or was that the heat from the heavy length of his body that was burning into hers?

"Um," she said, licking her lips and looking up at him. He didn't move. She didn't ask him to.

He felt good. Heavy, masculine and hard. She had to force herself not to widen her thighs and arch against him. It was almost embarrassing.

Except that he seemed to be having the same trouble—more so because he couldn't hide his reaction, his heavy shaft pressing into the crux of her thighs.

"Don't do that," he said, his breath sounding short.

"Don't do what?"

"Lick your lips like that."

"Oh, sorry," she said, not sounding sorry at all. She couldn't help but notice that he hadn't moved yet.

"I should probably get up," he said, his breath warm on her cheek.

"Yeah."

"But I really don't want to," he admitted, and she might have imagined it, but it seemed that he pressed himself against her thigh ever so slightly.

Heat streamed through her, making her wet and

all too close to the edge. All he'd have to do is edge one of those thighs down in between—or any part he wanted—and she'd be gone.

Resisting temptation never had been one of her strong suits.

He dipped in suddenly, fusing his lips to hers, diving his fingers into her hair and wiping her mind clean of anything but him.

The surprise of it shook her, and Joanna opened underneath him, her lips parting, her thighs opening, her arms sliding around his massive torso as she gave herself over.

For the first time in her life, she knew what it was like to be truly carried away by the moment. By a kiss. By a man.

"This is better than I even imagined," he whispered into her ear, taking a break to catch a breath, and drawing the tip of his tongue along the lobe.

Joanna had to bite her lip hard to stop from moaning in pleasure at the contact.

"So you've been fantasizing about me, huh?" she said, trying to reach for something light, something to ward off the intensity that had exploded between them.

"From the second I saw you," he admitted, much to her surprise, as he drew back and looked straight down into her face. She could tell by his eyes that he wasn't lying.

His gaze dropped to her mouth. She wanted him to kiss her again almost more than she wanted to breathe, and that scared the daylights out of her. As much as she enjoyed sex, usually men wanted her more than she wanted them.

"Maybe we should get up now," she said, trying to

control her voice and her breathing as something close to panic set in.

She didn't know why; she wanted him, and she wasn't afraid of him. But at the same time as her body was screaming for him, her mind was sending out red alerts.

"Are you sure?" he asked, not moving.

His hand slid up the side of her rib cage, his thumb moving lightly over a nipple, making her suck in a breath and arch, even though she tried to stop her reaction.

"You're my boss," she said, unsure what relevance that would have, but apparently she'd hit the right key.

He stilled, pressed up tight against her, staring down.

"I would never use that. Not in this way," he said seriously, his hand dropping to the side of her. "Not at all. In fact, I've never slept with anyone I worked with, though I have to admit, none of the people I worked with were as hot as you."

"I—I didn't mean it like that. You don't…seem like the type to coerce someone into sleeping with you. It's just that…it can make things complicated."

"Yeah, sometimes. Is there someone else? Are you worried about your ex?"

"No to both," she said, knowing that she was just opening the door she really should be closing.

"Good," he said, looking down at her intently. "I'm fine with being your in-between. Your rebound guy," he said, leaning down to nuzzle her throat in a way that made her melt again. "We could have some fun," he promised. "No strings attached. At work, it's just work. No pressure."

So, so tempting.

Joanna wasn't sure she wanted to say no. What was the harm, after all?

Then he lifted away from her, and the heat of his body was replaced with the blasting air of the AC hitting her directly.

Callahan stood by the side of the bed, extended a hand. She ignored it, and rolled to standing, fixing her clothes. She didn't catch herself in time to prevent a wince as she rolled over her still sore shoulder.

"What's wrong?"

"Nothing."

"Your shoulder, you hurt it."

Thank goodness the T-shirt she wore hid the scar from the bullet wound. She covered it up with makeup when she wore anything revealing, but she knew he'd recognize it for what it was. Thank God he hadn't managed to get her shirt off. She kicked herself for forgetting, but it was a good reminder of why this couldn't happen.

"I tweaked it carrying a heavy load of dishes, that's all."

"You could let one of us get the really heavy trays."

"Sure. I will next time," she said cooperatively, which made him narrow his eyes.

"I think it's not a good idea. You know, us, hooking up," she added.

Looking him in the eye, it took no small amount of discipline not to let her gaze slip lower.

"Sure, whatever you want."

They stood there, facing each other until she turned and walked out of the room. He followed, not saying a word. In the front room, comforted by the brighter light from the lamp, she wrapped her arms around herself, still warm and aroused, trying not to focus on how amazing he looked.

He smiled a little, killing her, and walked to the door. “Let me know if everything is okay with the AC, and, you know…if you change your mind.”

She smiled, nodding, and didn’t dare say a word in case she asked him not to go. When he was gone, she fell back into the chair and thought the next few weeks might not be quite as easy as she thought.

3

Ben knew that Joanna was right. It probably wasn't a good idea for them to get together, but after having her under him, he was only interested in getting her naked and in bed. He was pretty sure smart had nothing to do with it. He was also sure she wanted him just as much, and while they could back off for a while, if she stayed on here, it was going to happen.

He checked in on the band as they were doing their sound checks and visited with a few people across the room, the crowd thickening as the hour passed. Business would be good tonight.

Louis, the extra weekend bartender, was on drinks and Ben wondered where Charlie was. Heading back to the kitchen, Ben walked over to the huge pot on the stove where Charlie's secret-recipe chili was bubbling away. Large pans of corn bread were cooling on the massive wooden block that dominated the center of the cooking space. That would be the only item on the menu tonight. Thursday through Saturday were specials-only nights. Most of the crowd was there for drinking and dancing, anyway.

Ben had no idea what his friend did to that chili, and Charlie wouldn't tell anyone, but it was the best Ben had ever had in his life. It would be gone before the night was over, and Ben made a mental note to make sure he snagged a bowl or two before he went back to the house.

Charlie and Lisa would handle the night shift, giving Ben the evening off. Tonight, though, he was antsy, and he would rather have stayed busy.

He moved toward his office, the idea of balancing books was probably the only thing that could calm his desire after leaving Joanna. On the way, he heard some curious noises and stilled, listening closer.

After a moment, he realized he was hearing lusty sounds of sex that were quite identifiable and coming from the employee lounge. A female voice cried out, obviously too excited to keep mute, quickly followed by chuckling and whispers.

Charlie and Lisa, he realized, with no small bit of shock. Obviously thinking they were alone and taking a quick break out back.

Ben wasn't sure how he felt about that. Or, rather, he was fine—glad even—about his friends getting together, but break-room sex was a little…brazen. Not to mention breaking several health codes, he thought with a smile.

Maybe he was just jealous since he and Joanna hadn't managed to close the deal. He'd happily break a few health codes with her. Taking a breath, he decided to bypass his office and head straight back out to the house. He didn't want Charlie and Lisa knowing anyone had heard them. If they hadn't said anything, it was because they wanted to keep whatever they were doing a secret. That was their business.

Needing to work off some steam, he ran upstairs in the two-story cabin and grabbed his shorts and running shoes.

He didn't bother warming up but hit the side of the long road heading away from the Lucky Break running full-out. His body welcomed the punishment, and he pushed it harder in the second mile, muscles burning, but the nice rhythm that eventually set in calmed some of the agitation from the encounter with Joanna.

Not that any amount of exercise could equal the satisfaction he imagined he could find in her arms, but it would have to be close enough, since he was at an impasse.

Lost in his thoughts, he slowed down in the third mile and cast a glance backward as he noted an SUV behind him, in the distance. No problem. The sun was still up and he was easily visible. Drivers around here were always on the lookout for cattle or any wild animals that happened onto the road, especially at dusk.

To be extra safe, however, Ben moved over onto the sandy dirt on the side, keeping his pace as he heard the engine noise grow closer.

Pacing his breathing with his steps, he ignored the tingling at the base of his neck at first, something he'd always counted on as a SEAL as a sure sign that there was a problem.

The car had slowed down. Two people in the car. It hung back slightly. He slowed, and then heard the engine gun.

"Let's see what's going on," Ben said to himself and turned right, heading off into the desert landscape, running toward a dune that would be too steep even for a vehicle outfitted for sand, which this one wasn't.

He picked up the pace, closing the half mile to the dune, and sure enough, looked behind to see the SUV speed up, leaving the road and taking chase.

Ben knew every feature of the local landscape like the back of his hand, and as the sun started to lower on the horizon, shadows stretched over the ground and he hoped that would give him an advantage.

The SUV had four-wheel drive, and while it wasn't doing as well negotiating around rocks and brush as Ben was, it was closing the distance between them too quickly. Ben headed up the sand hill and ignored the burning in his calves that told him he wasn't working out as hard as he should be. He made a mental promise to start getting off the road and running across the mountains daily. Civilian life was no reason to become soft.

He made it to the top as the sun was dipping down under the horizon. With the advantage of cover and higher ground, he saw the SUV plow into the base of the dune, unable to follow.

"Now you'll have to get out on foot, idiots," he muttered, ducking down behind a fallen tree trunk to wait.

There were numerous other things to worry about in the desert as night fell, but for the moment, the two men who slammed the car doors shut and started up the dune were his biggest concern.

He could slide down the other side, circle around and get the car, leave them stranded. But he wanted to know who they were, and he wanted to make sure they wouldn't be back.

Watching one guy silently tell the other guy to split

directions, Ben smiled to himself. Individually, he could take them both pretty easily.

Staying low, he went for the bigger one first. If he had the drop on that guy, it wouldn't be hard to convince the other to give up.

They weren't even wearing boots, he observed, watching one stop to dump sand out of what was probably an expensive dress shoe.

Doubling back over the top of the dune, Ben walked nearly silently, until he was standing behind the big man, who had his gun drawn. Ben poked him on the shoulder, and the guy jumped, surprised.

The gun went off, and Ben wasted no time grabbing the guy's firing arm—controlling the hand that held the gun was always the first priority—and followed up with a hard left-cross that threw the guy backwards down the hill. His gun flew out of his hands as he tumbled down to the bottom, where he lay motionless.

Ben slid down the sandy face of the red sand dune feet-first, focused on his prey, not noticing the pain and abrasions his arms and legs were sustaining on the way down.

Grabbing the unconscious man, Ben confirmed that he was still living and grabbed his wallet, checking for what was inside: the ID was clearly fake, and Ben threw it back to the dirt. The car was a rental, though he noted the plate and rental company.

Moments later, he heard the labored breathing of the other guy approaching from the opposite side of the truck. Ben wasn't the only one who needed to get in better shape, apparently.

The other assailant came around the back of the car.

Ben slammed him hard, his gun going off before he dropped it and Ben got an arm lock on his throat.

"Who are you?" Ben demanded.

"Did you kill him?" the guy asked, sounding young and staring at the first guy, who was still out cold.

Ben didn't respond, letting the guy's fear work for him, squeezing a little tighter. One good twist and he would snap the man's neck, though he had no intention of doing that. His prey didn't know that, however.

The guy tried to fight, unsuccessfully, wheezing out a breath as Ben tightened his grip.

"Who. Are. You? And who sent you?" Ben asked again.

"Don't know," the guy huffed out. "We—we were hired anonymously, through contacts, you know? They gave us a picture, a location, said make it look like an accident. That's all I know."

Ben was inclined to believe him. The thug was young and had cracked too quickly under pressure.

"You need to find a better line of work, kid, before you end up dying young," Ben said. "Get your buddy, leave, don't come back, or you won't get a second chance. Got it? You can pass that on to whoever hired you, too."

Ben released his grip and slid backwards quickly in a move he knew would make it seem as if he had melted into the dark.

Ignoring the road, he took a long diagonal across the scrub desert back toward his house.

When he heard the car start behind him in the distance, the engine noise roaring off in the opposite direction, he relaxed and finished the walk, suddenly aware of his scraped, abraded skin.

Finally reaching his house, he walked in the back door and closed it, gulped a couple of glasses of water and took in the scrapes and bruises he'd acquired. Nothing too serious, though he had some of the other guy's blood on his favorite running shirt. Must have hit him harder than he thought.

As he headed to the shower, he was stopped by a knock on the door, and he paused. Music was now blasting from the roadhouse, and he wondered if the two men in the desert had followed him. Sometimes customers, having drunk too much, wandered back to his house, thinking they could use the bathroom or whatever, and he had to send them back to the bar. Peering through the curtain at the edge of the room, he was surprised to see it was Joanna, his tension dissolving.

When he opened the door, she opened her mouth to say something, but stopped, her eyes widening as she took him in.

"What happened to you?"

"Went for a run in the desert, took a misstep. What's going on?" he asked, stepping aside so that she could come in.

"I was just going to ask if you minded me adding on another shift. Charlie and Lisa can barely keep up in there, and he called me down, but I thought I should check with you first," she said, still taking in his appearance.

Tight black jeans and a black T-shirt hugged her shape, and he took in every inch, almost forgetting the events of the past hour. The silver and turquoise earrings she wore gave her an earthy, exotic look that made him want to pull her in and close the door, but instead he nodded.

"Yeah, definitely. Let me get cleaned up and I'll be over to help as well. Usually three is enough for Thursdays, but I should have figured it would be busier with these guys playing," he said.

"Great, thanks," she said simply and turned, walking back to the roadhouse.

Once he closed the door again, what had happened out on his run came back with a vengeance.

The danger was real. If they knew about him, they probably knew about his parents, who lived just down the road, and his friends. Lisa and her kids—anyone who mattered. The realization only drove home for him how important it was for him to stay close. If he reported this to the marshals, they'd take him into custody, and leave his parents, Charlie, Lisa out here, alone. So he'd keep it to himself.

His next thought was of Joanna. This was not a good time to get into any kind of relationship—not that sleeping with her meant that they were in a relationship, per se. Still, anyone close to him was in danger, and that wasn't fair to her. Not after what she'd just been through with the jerk that she'd left behind.

Ben would make sure no harm came to her either way, whether from outside, or due to his interest in her. He had the marshal's number, but for now, he'd continue to take care of the situation himself.

He stepped out of the shower, wincing at a particularly sore scrape on his upper thigh. Bandaging it, he pulled on jeans and a black button-up, heading over to the bar. The deep bass beat of a popular country-rock tune vibrated through the ground as he walked from one door to the other, and he couldn't help but look forward to seeing Joanna again, no matter what was going to happen—or not—between them.

JOANNA HOPED THAT BEN DIDN'T check with Charlie about her story. She'd actually suggested to Charlie that she take an extra shift, and then she'd gone over to talk to Ben on her own.

She told herself it was because she wanted to keep an eye on him. From her apartment window, she'd seen him take off running on the highway, but hadn't seen him return. He'd left far too quickly for her to try and follow, and she'd been pacing the floor, waiting for him to return.

Obviously he had come back, and he looked as if he'd had something more than a fall happen—or it had been one heck of a tumble. There was no reason to doubt his story, except that her gut told her he was holding something back. That wasn't enough to act on, though. Certainly not enough to warrant a call to Don. Maybe if she could get closer, talk to Ben, get inside his house, she could find out more.

As the evening wore on, she could tell he had taken her seriously. Ben was polite and friendly, but he kept his distance. No more hot looks as they all worked together to provide drinks and sustenance for the energetic groups of dancers and partiers at the bar.

Finally, after a blur of hours and movement, she collapsed tiredly into a chair by the bar, unsure if she could make it upstairs or not.

"Wow," was all she could say, and then said it again when Lisa handed her a wad of cash from the divided tips. Louis had left around midnight, as soon as the band shut down, and it was just the four of them cleaning up.

Lisa grinned. "It was a good night. Thanks for the help."

"No problem. With tips like this, I could quit—"

She cut herself off quickly, causing Lisa to look at her curiously.

"Quit what?"

Joanna smiled, recovering from her slip. It would have been a very, very bad slip, but she was exhausted. Her near revelation of her real job proved it was time for her to go to bed.

"Quit looking around for something better," she adlibbed. "I wasn't sure I could earn enough to stay here for long, but this changes my mind. Maybe I could even afford a place of my own eventually."

Lisa nodded. "You're a good worker. If you decide to stay on, we'd be happy to have you. Ben, particularly, I think," she said with a sly grin.

"Why would you say that?" Joanna asked, not making eye contact as she pushed up from the chair.

"Don't play games, Joanna. It doesn't take a genius to know he's interested in you, and let me tell you, he hasn't been interested in anyone else since he got back," Lisa added seriously. "I know you've had a hard time, too, but Ben's a good guy."

"Are you warning me off?" she said, looking up with a smile. She didn't take any offense to Lisa feeling protective of Ben. She'd known him for a long time, from what Joanna could tell.

"No, just letting you know, Ben's a straight-shooter. He doesn't play games, and I just thought you should know that. Sometimes when you've been with someone who messes with you—and believe me, I know—it's hard to tell the good guys from the bad guys anymore."

"You're right, thanks. I kind of figured he's one of the white hats, but I don't know that I'm ready to take up with anyone just yet," Joanna replied honestly.

"Sometimes it happens whether you're ready for it or not," Lisa said softly, her eyes drifting over to where Charlie stood talking to Ben as they put the liquor bottles behind the bar in order.

"You and Charlie, huh?" Joanna asked.

Lisa jumped, and realized she'd been caught. "Yeah, but it's…new. I'm not even divorced yet, so we haven't been public about it."

"You can count on me not to say a word," Joanna promised, and made a mental note to check into Lisa's husband's background as well. "But if you don't need me anymore right now, I'm going to go to bed and probably sleep through the next day or two," she joked, knowing she had to be up and ready for the lunch shift the next day.

"I hear ya. It's okay now, in the summer. My mom takes the kids on my late nights, but when school starts, I'll only be able to do Friday and Saturday. That's why I'm so happy we have you—it takes a real load off for all of us," Lisa said with an appreciative look. "Finding good, reliable help isn't easy these days."

Joanna squelched the pinch of guilt that the comment brought, smiling and saying good-night as she stretched her arms over her head and then headed for the stairs.

She hadn't done too much undercover work over the years. Mostly, she chased down bad guys out in the open and took them to jail when she caught them.

This was different. There were no bad guys in sight,

and she was lying to the good guys. It bothered her more than she wanted it to.

Less than three weeks, more like two and a half, and she'd be out of here. She was quite sure Lisa and Ben would find another waitress to take her place, and life would go on.

As she walked up the stairs and into her apartment, she went directly to the very-chilled-down bedroom, turned the AC to low and fell into bed, coming immediately awake as the memory of her and Ben here on the bed just a few hours ago came back to her in an erotic flash.

Groaning in frustration, she pushed back off the mattress and stripped down, heading into the small, square shower. Opening the little window high on the wall, she turned on the water and stepped in.

Thoughts of Ben followed her. His strong shoulders, the way he had weighed her down into the bed, his erection pressing into her thigh.

We could have some fun. No strings attached.

Joanna ran the bar of soap over her skin and closed her eyes, picturing Ben, and thinking about what could have happened if she had just said yes.

One simple little word, and she could have known what it was like to be with him.

Running a hand over her breasts, she teased her nipples, remembering how he had touched her.

Letting one hand slide lower, she fantasized about how he'd look without those jeans on, how big he'd be, and how he'd feel sliding deep inside of her.

Within seconds a deep, throbbing climax had her shaking, leaning back against the shower wall and crying out as she let every image loose in her imagination. Driving herself up one more time, she found her pleasure easily a second time, and then collapsed forward, the hot spray raining over her.

As her hand fell to her side, momentary satisfaction was replaced with a frustrating sense of it not being enough.

Not *nearly* enough.

But it would have to do, she told herself ruthlessly as she finished washing, dried off and walked out to the bed, exhausted.

Lisa was right, she thought sleepily as she began to doze off. Ben was a good guy, a white knight. He deserved better than someone being with him under false pretenses, even when it was her job. Even when she was keeping him safe.

She couldn't afford the distraction, and he deserved more than her lies.

Maybe…when this was over?

Maybe after his appearance in court, when she wasn't working here and could be honest about who she was. Maybe then, they could spend some time together.

The delusion vanished as quickly as it had arisen. If—or rather, when—Ben discovered who she really was, she figured he wouldn't be so crazy about her then.

She was here to do her job, not to sleep with Ben Callahan. Even so, fantasies of what could have been followed her into a restless night's sleep.

BEN STOOD OUTSIDE THE BAR FOR a long time. He'd taken out some bags of trash and stopped to pick up a few beer bottles ditched at the edge of the parking lot when he'd looked up and seen the light go on in Joanna's window.

It wasn't like him to stand outside a woman's room gawking, and he didn't know why he did it now, but he did. Standing still in the dark, he heard her turn on the shower.

The window was too high for him to achieve true Peeping-Tom status, but he waited there, listening to the water, imagining what she'd look like with the wet spray cascading down over her body, driving himself completely crazy.

Then he heard something other than the sound of the water floating down, clearly the soft cry of a woman in climax rising over the rain of the shower.

The idea of Joanna up there, alone in the shower, touching herself that way nearly dropped him to his knees right there on the pavement. He wanted nothing more than to go up and join her.

Aching, hard as a rock with wanting, he forced himself to walk back to his house instead of up to her room. He didn't bother turning on the lights as he made his way upstairs, stripping down and falling on top of the blankets, not even bothering to cover up.

The echo of her moans teased his mind, and he wanted to be the one giving her that pleasure. Wanted to bury himself deep inside her, taste her, touch her and take her in every way he could imagine. He could imagine a lot.

Remembering how she'd felt beneath him, how quickly her nipple had hardened under his fingers, how soft her mouth was, he closed his eyes and pictured her in that shower. In his mind's eye, he was there with her. A few quick strokes later, the release he found offered minor relief, but paled in comparison to how he knew it could be with Joanna.

After the trial, he promised himself in the dark.

After the danger had passed and his testimony was done, he'd go to her again, and this time, they'd find their satisfaction together. Not alone, like this.

It was only a few weeks, and then they could be together. The thought was enough to let him sleep, even though another part of his mind taunted him that he'd never be able to wait that long.

4

"NICE OF YOUR MOM TO TAKE THE kids," Charlie said, grinning wickedly and diving back under the covers to slide his hands up Lisa's shapely legs, parting her thighs and making her arch off the bed in a way he loved to make her do.

It was a rare opportunity, a whole night together, the chance to wake up together in the morning. He was exhausted, and so was she, but neither of them felt like wasting the moment. He never spent the night at her place because of the kids and because of her husband threatening her bid for full custody.

So their time together had consisted of stolen moments, times when they could sneak off and be together for a few hot, heady bouts of lovemaking. Not that he was complaining, but the prospect of waking up with Lisa in the morning had him so excited he could hardly sleep.

He found ways to keep busy, enjoying her cries of satisfaction as he made her come again, and then moving up over her to slide home and find his own, too.

Later, he pulled her close, kissing her hair.

She was the best woman he'd ever known. The fact that she'd fallen for him, with his one leg and not much else to offer a woman, proved that. Or maybe she just had a thing for lost causes. He wasn't going to look at it too closely.

She didn't deserve any of the hard things life had tossed her way, and Charlie wanted to give her everything else, all of the good things she deserved.

"That was nice," she murmured sleepily, her hand draped across his chest.

"Nice?" he asked in mock surprise. "All you have to say for all of my efforts is that it was nice? I guess I'll just have to try harder," he declared, lifting the blankets as if to go back under, but she stopped him, laughing.

He loved how her eyes lit up when she laughed.

"No, no, I mean it was *very* nice. Amazingly nice. Just like you," she said, her hand to his face, drawing him back next to her. "If-you-do-it-again, I-might-have-a-heart-attack nice."

He smiled. "That's better." But then he sighed and pulled her in closer. "It *was* nice. So is this."

"Yeah, it is."

"No word from your lawyer yet?"

"Just the bill. But no, Paul is still trying to get shared-custody, and I'll be damned if I let that happen. No way can he have those kids except under supervised visitation. Not the way he drinks," she said, and he regretted bringing it up, feeling her body tense next to his.

Paul had beat Lisa when he was drunk, and she'd kicked him out when he'd started turning his anger on the kids.

Personally, Charlie would like to take care of the

problem himself. Drive over to Midland, have a little heart-to-heart with the man and show his face the pavement if necessary. Get him to step away from Lisa in any way he could.

But he knew that wouldn't help. In the end, the bastard would only use it against her. Paul had a good job, though how he kept it was anyone's guess, and he could afford a lawyer who fought for his "rights" with his kids. Charlie was giving her every cent he could to help pay for a lawyer just as good, but it was slow going.

He had to be patient. Lisa was his, and he'd protect her in any way he had to, and if that meant not fully being part of their lives for now, that was okay. He spent time with her and the kids. They liked him; he thought so anyway, and he loved them like his own. It would happen, sooner or later.

Maybe they'd have a few more of their own, he thought, the well of emotion nearly bursting in his chest.

"Oh, I almost forgot," she said, turning over and pushing up on one elbow. "A guy stopped by the house for you."

His sleepy, relaxed state changed quickly. No one knew about him and Lisa, not even Ben. Charlie hadn't been willing to risk it, just in case Paul found out. No one should be looking for him at her house.

His gut sank, because he knew who it was before she spoke.

"Yeah? When was that?"

"Evening before last. I'm sorry, it just completely slipped my mind. The kids were driving me crazy, and then there was work, and I—"

"Did he say who he was?" he interrupted.

"He just said to let you know Joe had come by, and wondered if you had finished the job. Are you working on a bike for him?"

Charlie made extra money on the side refurbishing motorcycles. He didn't ride anymore, but he enjoyed working on them.

"Yeah. I guess I must have mentioned you to him. Sorry about that," he said, his gut twisting.

Joe wasn't waiting for a bike. Joe was a part of Charlie's past he'd rather forget, a part that had come back to haunt him. Charlie had assumed it had gone away, that if he just let time pass, they'd leave him alone. But they had been watching, apparently.

This was more than a visit, it was a message. He hadn't told them about Lisa—no way—but they were letting him know that they knew. Knew about the two of them, knew that she was important, and that they could walk right inside her house if they wanted.

He pulled her in as she began to snore softly in his arms. He'd do anything—*anything*—he had to in order to protect her and the kids.

This time, that could come at a very high price.

It could cost him his best friend. Charlie knew the secret Ben was keeping—the men who'd threatened him told him what had happened at the rodeo, and that Ben hadn't been out of town last week to check on a problem with their liquor distributors. Well, he had, but he was also meeting with the feds about a murder he'd witnessed. Knowing his friend was going through that ate Charlie up inside. Still, Ben hadn't come to him, either.

He had to put Lisa and the kids first. Ben would understand, but hopefully, he'd never have to find out what Charlie knew, or what he'd been asked to do, if only Charlie could find a way out of it.

For now, he would lose his mind in Lisa, and leave the rest for later.

JOANNA NEARLY MOANED OUT LOUD as she bit into the thick turkey club that Lisa gave her as they sat at a small table after the Friday lunch hour.

Now the Lucky Break was quiet again as the bulk of the lunch crowd was gone. The sandwich had thick slices of avocado, her favorite, and she smiled in deep pleasure at the mix of flavors in her mouth. Sex might not be an option for her right now, but the food around here was so good it was almost making up for it.

"Heaven," she murmured as she swallowed and grabbed her soda.

"Nothing sexier than a man who can cook," Lisa said with a grin, her eyes drifting over to Charlie.

"That would be nice," Joanna said with a wistful smile. "One skill I never quite picked up."

Lisa grinned. "Me neither, actually. The kids love when Charlie makes dinner."

Joanna lifted her glass. "To men who can cook."

Lisa met her glass with a nod.

"So why are you guys so on the down-low with this? Charlie seems like a solid guy, and you might not be divorced, but you're separated."

"It's more complicated when you have kids, and Paul is trying to get custody. I can't do anything that he could take to court to prove I am not a fit full-time parent."

"Jerk. He hit you?"

Lisa stared, clearly surprised. "Why do you say that?"

In her line of work, Joanna knew too much about what bad men did to women, and could see it in their faces even if they didn't say a thing. Of course, she couldn't tell Lisa that.

"Been there," she said instead, though that wasn't true. If a guy ever tried to hit her, he'd be out before he knew what hit him back.

"Yeah, and I put up with it, thinking it was better for the kids to have both parents at home. My folks were divorced, and so many of the kids' friends are from broken homes, too—"

"The way I see it, their home was more broken with him around. Kids know, believe me."

Joanna remembered hearing her parents fight before her mom had left. She didn't know what it was about, she was too young to understand, but she knew the tension in their house that kept her in knots. She also knew how it went away and things were better when her mom was gone, hard as it was.

"Thanks," Lisa said with a small smile. "But, I only went to the E.R. once, so there isn't much of a record of it. And Ben's grandpa, who helped me a few times, is passed on now, so you know, there aren't many witnesses to convince the court."

"He didn't hit the kids?"

"He was heading that way. I kicked him out and got a restraining order before he did any real damage."

Joanna sat back, making another mental note. She might be able to help here, though she couldn't say anything now. She could see why Lisa was cagey about Charlie, though. It also meant Lisa was vulnerable, and that if someone wanted to get access to Ben, she would be a ripe target.

"Hey, where's Ben?" she asked Lisa, changing the subject. She'd have time later to look deeper into Lisa's ex, and she should probably look a little closer into Lisa, too, to make sure there wasn't a possible problem there.

But Joanna hadn't seen Ben all day, and while she knew she couldn't keep eyes on him every second without blowing her cover, when it went past a few hours, her own alarm bells started chiming.

"He was over to his parents' ranch all morning helping get ready for the party tomorrow."

"What party?" Joanna asked. Ben's parents' ranch was on the same land as the Lucky Break, all part of the family business. The main house was about ten miles down the road.

"He didn't tell you?" Lisa said, frowning.

"Nope. I assumed tomorrow was a regular work day, but there's a party here?"

"Not here. We're closed for the day, and then we'll have Sunday off, too, as usual. This party is at his folks' place. His dad's fiftieth. They have a party every summer for his birthday. Everyone from everywhere comes around."

"Oh," Joanna said, feeling slighted that Ben hadn't told her, but also that she might not have a way to keep tabs on him for an entire weekend. That was a problem.

"I'm sure he meant to invite you, but things have been a bit busy," Lisa said, looking at her knowingly.

"It's no problem. So he's out there all day today?"

"I think he got back an hour or so ago, and headed upstairs with his tool belt. He said he needed to fix something electrical. You were busy with customers, so I guess he just went up."

Joanna froze. Ben was in her apartment, alone?

She was careful, but she didn't count on people being in her space when she wasn't there. She'd left her phone there as well as her extra gun.

"I'm going to go see what he's doing," she said quickly, pushing away from the table. "You okay here?"

Lisa chuckled. "Yeah, I'm fine. You go see what he's up to. Maybe he needs a hand," she said lightly, her eyes dancing, clearly assuming Joanna was headed upstairs hoping to meet Ben for a little afternoon delight.

Joanna wanted to make sure he wasn't looking around her apartment when she wasn't there. Why he would, she didn't know, but given his background, it wasn't untenable that he might want to know more about her than she was telling him.

Upstairs, she found the door cracked open, and stepped inside to see Ben's tools and belt on the floor near one of the wall sockets that had been taken apart, but there was no sign of Ben. She heard a knock, something hitting something else, and a groan. Definitely male.

Her heart rate picked up, and she grabbed the gun she had put in the ankle holster she'd worn under her jeans—she always carried it in one spot or another—and moved it to the small of her back, where it was more accessible.

Moving through the apartment, she walked along the edge of the wall. Had someone followed him up here? Caught him unaware?

Moving one hand to her back, she entered the bedroom where she spotted the bathroom door ajar. Instinctively, she slowed her breathing, pausing for a moment.

Then she heard another clunk, and a cursing noise that had her across the room in a second, hand on the handle of the firearm at the base of her back as she flung open the door.

And found Ben rubbing his head as he looked up at her in surprise, soaked from head to toe, water spewing from a pipe in the wall. He bent back down, and turned the shut-off, killing the flow.

Joanna took a breath, relaxed, and set her hands on her hips.

"What are you doing?"

"Fixing your faucet," he said, as if that wasn't obvious.

"Why?"

"I was working on that faulty socket, until I had to use the facilities. I noticed it was leaking pretty steadily, and so I figured I could open it up, tighten up the coupling, but it didn't end up being that simple. The hardware was old, and the pipe was cracked, and—"

"And you just decided to do all of this without asking me?"

Her tone came out more sharply than she intended, but she was coming down from a state of high agitation, and had to take another breath.

"Well, you were busy, and this was the only time I had," he said, straightening and peeling off his wet shirt. "I remembered the socket had been a problem before, for Charlie, and, if you recall, I pay the water bill and the electric for this place. If something is broken, I'd appreciate knowing, especially something like plumbing."

She nodded, taking another breath. He was right, and she was being too touchy.

"You're right, sorry. I meant to mention it, but I didn't want to be a pest, especially after the air conditioning. The leak being a problem for you didn't even occur to me."

They both stood there in the small space, staring, her eyes drifting over his chest. There was only about two feet of space between them, and her shower fantasies were coming back to her with a vengeance.

"I, uh," she sputtered, stepping away before she did something stupid like jumping him right there and then, and bumped into the wall. She scraped the doorway on her way out and heard a heavy thud on the floor behind her.

Her gun.

Closing her eyes, she didn't turn around for a moment, knowing there was no way he'd missed that.

"What are you doing with *that?*" he asked, his tone low and dangerous.

Shaking her head, she turned back around, and reached for the weapon, but he made it to the Sig first.

"It's mine. I have a license," she said defensively.

"Why do you have it?" he asked again, stepping closer.

"I…a girl can't be too careful, you know? I picked it up in San Diego."

"Most women who have a gun leave it in the night stand, or somewhere in their house. Maybe in their bag. They don't usually carry," he said, and dipped down before she could stop him, running a hand over her shin, feeling the leg holster, and looking at her curiously.

"Tell me about this, Joanna. Now."

She fell back on her cover story. Thank goodness she had invented her lousy ex, Lenny.

"I was more worried about Lenny showing up than I said before," she said, biting her lip. "Or any of his friends. He carries, too, and I just wanted to make sure he didn't catch me off guard. I was afraid if I told you that before, you wouldn't keep me on."

Ben nodded. "I guess I can understand that, but you should have been straight with me."

"You're right. I'm sorry. I just like to handle things myself."

He looked down at the gun, moved it around in hands that obviously knew how to handle weapons.

"You know how to shoot?" he asked.

"Aim and pull the trigger," she said simply, making him smile.

"This weapon is heavy-duty. Have you fired it before?"

"The shop I bought it from had a target range. I used it once there."

He shook his head. "Meet me out back of my house in an hour."

She wrinkled her brow. "Why?"

"I can show you how to shoot, and not how to miss. You can get some practice there," he said, sticking the weapon in the back of his own jeans and reaching for his shirt.

"Hey!" she objected. "That's mine."

"It is. And when I'm satisfied you know how to use it well, you can have it back, but I don't ever want you carrying it on the floor again. You keep it here, with the ammo in a separate place. It's too dangerous, an amateur carrying a weapon around in a roomful of people," he added.

She wanted to rail, to tell him that she was no amateur. Far from it. Her training very likely prepared her to outshoot him, in fact. But she couldn't argue without blowing her cover, and besides, she still had her Glock under her pillow in the bedroom.

"Fine," she said sullenly as he moved past her in the small doorway, his bare chest only inches from her hands as he did so, which triggered another set of alarms in her head.

He smelled good, and she actually took a deep breath, looking up into whiskey-brown eyes that watched her back, just as intently.

"One hour?"

"One hour," she confirmed, and let out a breath as he passed by.

"I'll call someone to come by and fix that pipe," he added from the hall as she watched him gather his tools.

"Thanks."

Then he was gone, and she sank back to the bed, grabbing her Glock from under her pillow and seeking a better hiding spot where he wouldn't stumble onto that, too.

Not that he'd have any reason to go looking under her pillows, or be in her bed, but she couldn't risk it.

Looking around the apartment, she finally settled on the top shelf of an empty kitchen cabinet. No one would have a reason to be searching there, not even Ben. She could put the gun back under her pillow at night, so she had it close by, but during the day, no one would find it up there.

A beep from her phone caught her attention, and

she grabbed it from the bed, noting that the dossiers on Charlie and Lisa had come through, and she quickly dashed off a note asking for background on Lisa's ex, Paul, as well.

Scanning the documents, she saw nothing to be particularly concerned about in Lisa's file, not that she had expected anything. To be extra cautious, she replied asking for a list of recent calls to her phone, just to be sure.

Charlie's was a little larger, citing a few minor teenage troubles and then his military service. The only things that really caught her attention were some gaps in time after he'd left the VA. There was a lapse between when he'd left the hospital and when he had moved here with Ben, started working at the bar, not that that meant anything. He could have been staying with a friend or at a motel, in between times. Still, it made her want to look deeper. Unexplained time in someone's record could mean they were simply in between places to live, as she was now, or it could mean they were hiding something.

She was going to dig around Charlie's past, if for no other reason than that she was starting to like Lisa. While Charlie seemed like a good guy, if he was hiding anything, Lisa didn't deserve that, especially if her ex's lawyer discovered it first.

But that was for later.

Changing her clothes, Joanna washed up and prepared to go down and meet Ben, and hoped she could cover her training, convincing him that she didn't know how to shoot. That would be tricky. Shooting was as natural to her as breathing.

From a window, she saw Charlie in the parking lot,

talking to someone. It did not look like a friendly conversation.

Making her way quickly downstairs and out the back, Joanna slid along the side of the building, quieting her breathing and staying still near the corner where she heard the men's voices. They were using low tones, so she couldn't make out everything they were saying.

Charlie said something like "that was a mistake," Joanna heard, but then he lowered his voice before she could hear the rest.

"Yeah, well, you'd better listen up," the other man said.

"There's no way I'm…" Charlie responded with a hiss, and Joanna cursed under her breath, losing the second half of what he said to tires crunching across the gravel when a truck drove into the lot.

There was no way to tell if this was just a personal thing, or if it was a bigger problem, but she had to try to find out. Taking a deep breath, she stepped out from the edge of the building and smiled brightly as she approached the men.

"Charlie, there you are! I was looking everywhere for you," she said, joining them. She didn't miss how Charlie instinctively turned around and put himself between her and the other guy.

Protecting her? Or hiding the other man?

"What's up, Jo?" Charlie said, obviously stressed by her appearance.

"I wasn't sure about…whether you wanted the soup from lunch frozen or just put in the fridge."

It was thin, but all she could come up with.

"I'll do that when I come back in. Don't worry about

it," he said, giving her a look that clearly told her he wanted her to leave.

Joanna stepped to the side, and got a good look at the dark, towering man who watched them. He had goon written all over him, and obviously wasn't local. Certainly not a ranch worker—the hundred-dollar tie gave that away, as well as the shiny boots with hardly a speck of dust on them. For all of his fanciness, he still hit her as slimy.

The man glared, still as stone. Joanna looked from him to Charlie, and cocked her head, eyeing Charlie more closely.

"You sure you're okay?"

"Everything's fine," the dark man spoke smoothly, smiling in a way that sent shivers down her spine. "I was just trying to convince Charlie to convert over to a new security system for the bar," the man said. "Never can be too careful."

"Oh, you're a salesman," Joanna said, in feigned relief, then smiled.

"Yes."

"I know I said I'd consider buying, but I talked to my partner and we changed our minds," Charlie interrupted. "Thanks anyway. But it's not going to happen, so don't come back," he said to the guy emphatically, taking her by the elbow—a little too firmly—and turning away from the man without another word.

They walked back into the bar, and Joanna pulled her arm away. "Ow. Geez, Charlie," she exclaimed. "What was that all about?"

Luckily, Lisa was elsewhere.

"Sorry," Charlie said, still clearly anxious as he pushed a hand through his hair.

"Who was that guy? And don't bother lying. Anyone could tell he wasn't a salesman."

"You shouldn't have come out there," he said. "You could have gotten hurt."

"Who *is* he?" she demanded, on alert.

"A guy Lisa's ex sent to watch her, intimidate her. He came into the bar, looking for her, and I tossed him back out. I think he was at her house a few days ago. He's probably a P.I. or something, I don't know, but I don't want her knowing about it, and if he comes back, I'll handle it." Joanna wasn't sure what to think. Charlie seemed to be telling the truth, but even if he was, Joanna didn't think the man was a PI. He was far too threatening. He was there to intimidate, yes, and maybe worse.

"Okay, I won't say a word. Listen, I gotta go," she said, eyeing the clock, but planning to follow up as much as she could later.

"Thanks, Joanna. It's just…really difficult for Lisa, and I don't want her worrying more than she should. I can look out for her and the kids, and I don't want you getting in the middle or getting hurt, too."

"Thanks, Charlie," she said with a smile, though something was off. First, Ben was speckled with scrapes and bruises from a fall he supposedly took while running, and now some thug stood in the parking lot of his business, giving Charlie a hard time. There was no overt reason to think the two incidents were connected, but could Ben or Charlie be covering something up? She needed time to do some digging and find out, but right now she had to go convince Ben that she didn't know how to use a gun.

5

Joanna wiped her hands on her jeans, as if nervous, as Ben explained the basics of gun safety: always treat the gun as though it was loaded, even if you knew it wasn't. Always keep your finger off the trigger until you were ready to shoot. Don't point the gun haphazardly, and always know what was behind what you were shooting at—bullets traveled for a while, and you never knew what they'd hit.

She'd certainly seen enough accidental shootings during take-downs and drive-bys to know that last one could have the most tragic consequences of all.

Ben's target range was basic, but set up against the backdrop of a short, sandy bluff surrounded by trees and rocky outcrops that would catch any stray bullets, not that she expected that he missed often. Watching his hands expertly and confidently handle the weapon was almost erotic for her.

"Okay, I know you know how to shoot it, but actually hitting something you're aiming at is harder than you think," he continued.

She hoped she looked apprehensive as he handed her the gun.

"You comfortable with the slide? A lot of women have a hard time with it, but it's not so much muscle as technique."

"Yeah, the guy at the shop showed me how to do that. He sold a lot of his guns to women, I guess, so he had some tricks for doing it easily."

Ben nodded. "Awareness is the key. It might sound zen, but with guns, you have to be completely in the moment, completely aware of everything. Where your hands are placed, where it's aimed, the pressure you are exerting on any given part of the weapon, what's around you."

She looked away. Everything he said sounded sexual to her need-saturated brain, and she tried to focus. It was difficult as he wasn't telling her anything that she didn't already know, and her mind kept fixating on him.

"You can't be distracted by anything in your environment," he said. "You get too comfortable or forget to be aware of the power of the weapon, that's when bad things happen."

She couldn't be more aware than she was right now, not so much of the weapon, but of the man standing far too close, his big hands closing over hers as he repositioned her grip.

The touch sent her heart racing, and she didn't realize she was holding her breath.

"One more tip?" he offered.

"What?"

"Breathe. It's reflex to hold your breath, tense up, but you really have to relax into it, feel your body, your posture. Let the gun become part of your hand."

She smiled. "You sound more like a yoga teacher than a shooting instructor."

"You do yoga?" he asked, sounding interested, his voice close by her ear.

"Some," she said, trying to control her breathing, but his nearness was throwing her off.

That worked to her advantage in this case.

"Me too," he said, surprising her.

"So let's go over some basic stances, even though in defensive situations, most people shoot from whatever position they're caught in. What you're doing with your upper body is more important, but it's good to learn the basics, anyhow. They teach you balance and form," he said.

By the time he worked her through the three or four basic stances—using his hands to move her arms and torso, his foot to push her feet where they should be, sometimes edging his thigh against the inside of hers—Joanna wasn't sure she could hit a target if she tried.

Her hands shook slightly by the time she lifted the gun so he could show her how to aim. She was so turned on, though he likely thought it was nerves.

"You okay?" he asked, noticing.

"I think I was better off before—now I'm nervous about remembering all of this stuff," she said.

"You can come out and practice with me every day. You'll get better and the movements will be more natural. You'll be safer and everyone else will, too."

"So now I aim and shoot?"

"In a minute. Don't be in such a rush. Take your time." She heard the smile in his voice, though he was standing behind her. "Your sights on this have been pretty well adjusted, so you just need to know how to use them. They do that for you at the shop?"

She nodded.

"Well, you should learn to adjust them yourself, to account for windage and other factors, but we'll do that another time. For now, back to basics."

"What next?"

"Focus on this one, the front one," he said, and she took a deep breath, already lining up her shot reflexively. Her father had started teaching her to shoot when she was seven. She and Jarod had both garnered several youth marksmanship awards by the time she was fifteen, and the marshals had honed those skills to a fine point.

Joanna loved to shoot, and she even thought she might go into firearms instruction with the USMS sometime if she ever quit her job, but that wasn't going to happen for some time.

Still, her body wouldn't be denied, settling in as she lifted the gun into a familiar pose, her breath slowing and deepening as everything slowed down around her. Ben was talking and she knew she had to fight against her training, but it was hard.

Nature would help. There was a good wind coming from the west over the desert, and she knew how to throw her focus off very easily—closing her eyes, she thought about Ben behind her, his hands placed lightly on her waist, and how he could slide those hands over her front, touch her in ways she was dying for—

The blast went off, and she felt his hands grip her hips, helping her absorb the recoil. She let herself stumble back a little, as she might if she weren't used to it.

"What did I hit?" she asked, holding her hand up to

her eyes, letting her gun hand fall loose, the gun flailing around—she made sure her finger was off the trigger, but it was a common mistake with new shooters.

Ben immediately corrected her, taking the gun and reminding her to keep both hands on the weapon, her finger off the trigger, keeping it pointed at the target or the ground.

"Remember, you need to be aware all the time," he chastised gently, looking deeply into her eyes as if to drive the point home.

Oh, she was aware, all right. Her body was absolutely singing with awareness.

"Okay, sorry. It was just exciting. What did I hit?"

"That dead tree stump over there," he said, grinning.

It was yards off the target.

Mission accomplished.

"It would help a lot if you had opened your eyes," he added.

"How did you know I had shut them?"

"Rookie reflex, but you need to keep them open, both of them, not one, like you sometimes see on TV. You need your depth perception. Let's try again, and when you're done, keep the gun pointed but your finger off the trigger until you're ready to shoot."

She swallowed hard, aiming this time for a spot a little to the left of the center of one of the targets. She went wide—on purpose—but hit the background of the target.

"Way better," he said encouragingly, squeezing her shoulder. "Let's finish the clip. Take it slow, at your own pace."

She managed to spin a few more sexual fantasies of Ben, very handily throwing off her focus even as it aroused her to no end, but she'd have to deal with that later.

For the moment, she needed him to trust her with this gun so that he would let her take it back. She managed to get closer to the center of the target on the last two shots, and followed all the safety rules.

When the clip was empty, she turned, smiling brightly.

"That was fun, let's do some more," she said eagerly.

She needed to fire off another clip to work off some of the heat that lusting about Ben all afternoon was causing.

"Sure, you're doing great," he said enthusiastically, letting her reload on her own this time.

She made sure to mess up once or twice, taking deep breaths to steady her "nerves" and now and then sending a wild shot into the bluff. He corrected her grip, and she liked how his hands helped hers, guiding her actions.

Stepping back now, he left her on her own, and she managed to get one shot dead-on. Unable to help it—Joanna could only force herself to miss for so long, and it made sense that she might hit the target at least once, just according to the odds.

She did a girly hop, happy with her accomplishment.

Checking the safety was on, she handed him the gun in the way he had instructed her. He took it, looking at her with a warm smile.

"That was great, but why don't you show me how an expert does it?" she suggested, and stepped back, allowing him a chance to shoot.

He smiled, and she saw the glint in his eye that communicated his love of the sport as well as his acceptance of the challenge.

"Don't let this discourage you," he said. "I've been trained to do this, and I've been shooting for a long time."

"Don't worry, I know," she said, smiling widely from where she stood, several feet behind him.

When he took his position, adjusting the sights and finding his stance, she could have cared less about his shooting.

She was free to admire the effortless way he handled the weapon, and how the sun brought out reddish highlights in his gorgeous hair. She liked how his shoulders bunched as he lifted the Sig, and the play of muscles at the back of his neck, where she was so tempted to kiss him. Then he stilled and almost appeared to stop breathing as he unloaded several quick shots in a row.

All of them dead-center, almost on top of each other, blasting a single, huge hole in the center of the paper.

"That was…impressive," she said, and it was. She could match him, but she'd met few people who could shoot as well as she could.

He smiled, taking the clip out of the gun, making sure it was empty and putting the safety on before he holstered it.

"One of my favorite things to do. I have several firearms in the house. If you really like it, I can teach you to use them," he said.

She bent to help him clean up casings.

"I'd like that," she said.

He looked up when she did, and the strength of the attraction she experienced was like a magnet, made many times stronger by the afternoon of shooting and feeling him touch her, imagining all of the things she'd like to do with him.

When they stood, the next thing she knew she was plastered up against him, his arms so tight around her she thought she wouldn't be able to breathe. But she didn't care about that, as the kiss they were sharing was so encompassing that air was not a concern.

His hands were everywhere, in her hair, down her back, over her backside, pulling her tight against him and letting her feel that he was as turned on as she was.

She moaned into his mouth, wanting more, wanting to go deeper, to crawl inside him and have him inside her, too.

"I can't seem to keep my hands off you for long," he said, his hands now slipping up inside her T-shirt, running over her back, down her spine to rest at the edge of her jeans.

"I know, me neither," she confessed. It might be the first honest thing she'd said to him all day.

Then they were kissing again, and this time it was slow and deep, his tongue rubbing on hers, and she sucked him into her own mouth, feeling a groan rumble up from his chest as she did so.

The sun was setting low on the horizon. She had forgotten how long they'd been out here. When she drew back and looked at him, his ruggedly handsome face against the blue, blue desert sky, her heart flipped in a way she hadn't ever experienced before.

His hand came up to hold the side of her face, an achingly tender gesture that had her turning into his palm, kissing him there. She could smell the gunpowder mingling with his scent, and it aroused her even more.

None of this was acting. None of this was fake. She wanted him more than she wanted her next breath, and she realized she was willing to risk whatever consequences came with that—short of putting him in danger of course. But suddenly, taking in how he was looking at her, as if she was all he could see in the world, she was willing to risk him hating her later, losing her job, losing her heart. It would be worth it.

"Come out with me tonight," he said, jarring her focus. She'd expected him to ask her to bed, back to his house, but not...out.

"Where?"

"Dinner, someplace quiet, away from here."

"A date? Shouldn't we be at the bar tonight?" she asked, and then felt her face warm. She didn't date too often. Mostly she met guys she knew somewhere, and then they went home together. Sometimes not even that. Dating meant you were trying to get to know someone, maybe hoping for something more.

"Yeah, a date," he said, smiling. "I think they have enough help on tonight to spare us. You up for it?"

She smiled back, knowing she was making a critical mistake, but she wanted this. And she would be with him, which was the point of her being here, right?

"Yeah. Shooting works up an appetite," she said, the words coming out far more sexually than she intended, and in the space of a breath, they were kissing again for several more long, hot minutes, before they broke away, panting and smiling.

"Okay, I guess I should shower. I'll meet you up at your apartment in an hour or so?" he said.

She grinned. "Maybe I should meet you at your

car. We might not make it out of the apartment if you come up."

Desire, surprise and humor lit up his eyes as he laughed, nodding in agreement.

"Okay, I'll meet you at the car."

Joanna's heart was slamming as she walked back to her apartment, thinking about what she had in her meager suitcase to wear out to dinner. Dating wasn't something she had counted on. She caught Lisa on her way through the kitchen.

"Hey, I wonder if you might be able to help me out with something?"

Lisa, happy to be a coconspirator and apparently very happy to help her get ready for a date with Ben, met her back at her place a half hour later with several dresses.

"Here—you can keep these. After the kids, my shape changed a bit, and well…they'll definitely look better on you," Lisa said, laughing, though Joanna thought she looked in great shape.

"Thanks. I really appreciate it," she said with a smile, fully intending to give the borrowed clothing back at another point in the future, but it would come in handy now.

"You have fun," Lisa said with a wink, and Joanna went quickly through the clothes, finding a simple blue dress that she thought would work, neither too fancy nor too casual.

It fit her like a glove.

She went into her suitcase, dug out a delicate gold chain and fastened it around her neck. It was a graduation gift from her father that she only wore on special occasions. She always kept it with her, one of her most cherished possessions.

She paused, wondering what to do with her gun. She preferred to wear it, but for tonight, she'd put it in her bag. She had to keep it close, but the last thing she needed was Ben finding her carrying again. He'd have no reason to see inside her bag.

Ready, she took one last look in the mirror and headed downstairs to meet him, more excited than she expected she ever could be about going on a date.

BEN FOCUSED ACROSS THE SMALL table on Joanna, something he'd been unable to stop doing since they'd gotten in the car.

At the Lucky Break, she always looked good—always sexy in her short skirts and painted-on jeans—but tonight, she was elegant and classic in a pretty blue dress accompanied by a simple chain at her throat.

It occurred to him it was the first time he'd seen her with her hair down, and the way the silky strands moved over her shoulders was doing ferocious things to his libido.

She told him Lisa had lent her the dress, and the chain was a gift from a relative, but hadn't elaborated more than that. He didn't dig. Apparently she had painful things in her past, and he didn't want to unearth them tonight.

They sat in the back at a cozy Italian place he knew in Midland, where the food was good and the atmosphere was friendly and romantic. He'd wanted to sit near the window, but Joanna had preferred a table closer to the rear of the place. More privacy, she said.

He thought he caught her once assessing the space,

as if noting the exits and entrances, but when he asked, she told him she was looking for the restroom.

He felt like an idiot.

Still, there had been a moment while they were shooting, something that itched at his senses. Something in the way she stood when she took one of her shots, something in the way she moved that made him think she wasn't as new to marksmanship as she pretended.

Why would she do that?

Her shots had been off, but not too wildly after the first few, and she'd shown quick progress. He supposed what he had seen was potential—some people had natural talent for it—and she could be very good with practice.

"You seem deep in thought," she said, smiling at him over a glass of red wine. Her cheeks were warm from the drink and he hoped, from the company.

She was absolutely lovely, and he was a moron for sitting here thinking about shooting instead of romancing her into his bed at the end of the evening.

They could have headed straight there from the range, as hot as things were between them. They both wanted it, and the ruse of waiting was over. However, it was important to him to do more than take her back to his bed and work off a little steam. He wanted this—to spend some time getting to know her first. To have some time with her.

He wasn't going to think about why that was so imperative just yet.

"Just taking you in," he said honestly, and refilled both of their glasses. "You look pretty amazing."

"Thanks, but it's making me wonder what I must look like back at the bar," she responded with a grin.

"You always look good," he said. "Maybe too good, if all the guys who watch you are any indication."

"Good for tips," she quipped.

"Long as they keep their hands off," he said, also lightly, but feeling very possessive as he did.

"They do. Really, almost all of them are really nice, down-to-earth people. Several married and from your parents' ranch, as you already know," she said.

"Yeah. We run a tight operation, no smoking, no fights, no drugs. Granddad always ran the place that way. People come in to have fun, food, dance, but no trouble allowed."

"Having a former navy SEAL and a U.S. Army vet running the place probably helps with that," she offered as their salads arrived.

"Maybe. It was that way with my granddad, too—he didn't take any guff from anyone. I'm carrying on his tradition. It's always been a family kind of place."

"You were close with him?"

"Growing up, yeah. He was a huge influence on me. Told me stories of the battle at Normandy, and a few other major skirmishes in the Second World War that he was in."

"Navy?"

"No, army. But he definitely turned me on to the military at a young age."

"Your father serve, as well?"

"No, his life was the ranch. Still is."

"Nothing wrong with that," she said, digging into her salad plate, and he did the same.

"What about you? What did your parents do?"

She paused, and he remembered his vow not to dig into anything painful in her past.

"If you don't want to—"

"No, that's fine. My dad was a cop, and my mom took off when I was seven. My brother was older, and did his own thing. We were never too close, that's pretty much all there was to it," she said, shrugging and not meeting his eyes as she focused very tightly on buttering a piece of her bread.

He reached over, covered her hand with his. "I'm sorry you had a tough time of it. We don't have to get into it."

She took a breath, but was smiling when she looked up.

"It's okay, but I'd just rather talk about you. There's not much to say about me. I left home, tried college, went through a string of jobs and relationships, and now here I am. End of story," she said, shrugging again.

"What did you study in college?"

"Just liberal arts at first, you know, like everyone else who has no idea what they want to do," she said with a smile.

"Ever think of going back?"

She looked away, then grabbed her glass of wine and took a sip.

"What about you? College, or did you go straight in to the SEALs?" she asked, changing the subject back to him.

"I went for basic training, and then I did my college through ROTC, and I joined the SEALs after that."

"What did you study?"

"Engineering. I thought it might come in handy for operations and if I wanted to find some other job in the military after I was done with special ops. It's no help whatsoever in running a bar or fixing your plumbing, however," he said with a grin, wanting to put her at ease.

"Lisa said something about your dad's birthday tomorrow. Shouldn't you be over there helping, instead of out with me?"

The server interrupted them as their dinners arrived, giving him time to kick himself. He had completely forgotten to invite her to the party, though he had meant to mention it over the last few days.

When the server left, he shook his head. "I did what they needed me to do this morning, so no worries there. They have a lot of people on hand to help. But I do feel like an ass for forgetting to tell you—I meant to, but with one thing and another I've been busy, and—"

"It's no problem, Ben. It's a family thing. I understand, I didn't expect—"

"It is a family event, but it's hardly a family party. It's one of the summer's big things around here, and you are definitely invited. I even mentioned you to my parents, who insisted I invite you, but I dropped the ball," he said, hoping she realized he was telling the truth and not just inviting her after the fact.

"That's nice of you, but I don't want to intrude," she said, placing her napkin on her lap and slicing into a piece of succulent-looking chicken parmesan.

"You're not. This is completely my fault."

"Well, if you're sure," she said, smiling at him softly. "I don't have a gift for your father, though."

"He doesn't let anyone bring gifts—he doesn't want them, he just likes the excuse to throw a big bash, seriously. It would be his gift if you come and have a good time," he said, reaching to take her hand and stroking his thumb over the soft center of her palm. "Will I see you there?"

She smiled in a cute, kind of slanted way that he loved, and nodded. "Sure. But I'll bring something. Maybe we can at least pick up a card or your father's favorite whiskey or something on the way home."

Ben stopped stroking her palm. "How did you know my dad likes whiskey?"

"Just a guess. I saw some in your house, and figured you had to get your tastes from somewhere."

"Good guess. He does like a few of the upscale brands. I'll go in with you on a bottle. He'll love it."

"I can afford it now, Ben. I'm doing great with tips. Stop treating me like I'm some starving urchin you took in off the street," she said a little testily, drawing her hand back.

"Joanna, I didn't mean it that way. I don't think of you that way at all."

She set her fork down. "I know. I'm sorry, too. I'm just…wound kind of tight tonight, you know?"

The look she gave him was molten, and he knew what she meant. He was wound pretty tightly as well.

"Maybe we can have this packed up in a doggie bag to take back, and some dessert along with it?" he suggested.

Desire flickered in her eyes, and she nodded. "That sounds like a great idea."

An hour later, they were walking through the door of his house. Ben wanted to slow down, to pour her a glass of wine, set the lights or do something other than jump her the minute the door was closed, but he didn't need to worry about it, as things ended up.

As soon as the door was closed and he'd set the bag of takeout on the kitchen counter, she was on him, stealing the breath from him as her kiss told him in no uncertain terms what she wanted, and he was more than happy to give it to her.

6

"I LOVE YOUR HAIR," HE SAID, winding his hands through it, burying his face in her neck before returning to her mouth.

With one gulping breath, they sank back into each other again.

"I love your arms," she muttered against his mouth, sliding her tongue over his bottom lip, loving his taste as her hands delighted in the strong, corded muscles of his forearms, the thick mass of his shoulders.

At the moment, Joanna didn't care about anything but having him. She was tired of fighting, tired of wanting and not having. To hell with complications. It was so much nicer to think about the big man pressing her up against the counter, and how, by some miracle, he made her feel delicate. Sexy. Feminine.

It was something she didn't even know that she craved, until the instant Ben slowly slid down the zipper at the back of her dress, kissing her so softly while he did so that her toes curled.

And that was the miracle of it. She'd taken control,

started this hot and heavy, but he'd turned it around, grabbed control back by being gentle, seductive.

"Like silk," he murmured into her throat, nipping the flesh there and then kissing it as his hands ran over her.

She wanted him naked as quickly as possible, to return to the hard, pounding, mindless sex she'd decided to initiate.

Ben apparently had something different in mind.

She barely noticed as he maneuvered her away from the kitchen and over to the wide, antique divan that was on the other side of the room. She'd noticed it when she came in. It was a lush, sensual piece of furniture, clearly of Turkish or Persian origin. She'd thought it was a strange choice among the more standard, western furnishings of the rest of the ranch house, but then, nothing about Ben seemed to be predictable.

They stood in front of the divan, and she stopped his hand before he pushed the dress away. "Turn the lights off, or at least way down?" she asked.

She had covered up her scar, as usual, but she couldn't risk him discovering it. "I like the dark, it makes things more intimate," she added, meeting his eyes.

Actually, she loved the lights on. She wanted to see everything he did to her, watch him, but it was a risk she couldn't take at the moment.

He paused, but nodded. "Sure," he said and moved over to dim the lights very low before returning to kiss her. He eased the dress from her shoulders. This time she didn't stop him. The cushion of the divan gave beneath her as he lowered her down, never once breaking the kiss as he followed.

She imagined that she should be dressed in a filmy harem outfit, lying back on the luxurious cushion, ready to be taken by her handsome sultan.

"Too many clothes," he muttered, undoing her bra. Her fingers responded in kind, pushing his shirt off and running her hands over his chest. Some women might like men's butts or packages, but she was a chest and arms girl. A gorgeous male torso was all about strength and comfort.

For a second, they took each other in under the low, golden light in the room. He was beautiful, she thought, her heart slamming in her chest. Not overly built, but strong—clearly very strong. His hair and eyes were darker in the shadows. As he stared down at her with clear lust, looming over her with his powerful frame, she could easily imagine him a Persian king. *And she was his slave....*

Her exploring fingers found a jagged scar over his right rib. A knife wound of some sort? She drew her fingers over it as he shuddered under her touch. As she discovered that it wrapped nearly all the way to the middle of his back, her soft smile faded.

"What happened?" she asked.

"Training accident. Got caught on a wire fence," he said vaguely, and she knew he wouldn't—or couldn't—tell her more. She also doubted it had happened during training. She found another scar, something that felt a lot like hers—like a gunshot wound—low on his waist.

"This?"

"Not important," he said, taking her lips in a hot kiss and erasing any more questions.

Lying back, she closed her eyes, envisioning the divan surrounded by draping silk tied with gilded rope.

Relaxing, she let her arms fall back, her position receptive, open. They dispatched with the necessary disclosures quickly, and she was glad to know there was no need for barriers between them, wanting to experience him fully.

When she opened her eyes, she focused only on him, and saw heat flash in his expression.

"What are you thinking?" he asked.

Did she dare share her fantasy?

"It's this divan…it's so exotic. I was picturing you as a sultan," she said with a smile, hoping he didn't think she was an idiot.

Ben leaned down close, powerful arms bracketing her on either side as he trailed kisses from her shoulder up to her jaw and over to her lips.

"I guess that would make you my harem girl. My slave," he said, obviously very willing to play along.

"I guess so," she said on a gasp, her nipples beading as his chest hair caressed them. She sighed, arching her back for more.

"Touch me, then, slave," he said in a playful demand.

"Yes, master," she agreed, taking a submissive tone, sliding her hands down that amazing chest to undo his belt and then working the snap of his jeans quickly. She enjoyed his approving growl as she slid her hand down inside and wrapped her fingers around the hot, hard length of him.

"Oh, yesss," he hissed, pushing into her hand.

She paused briefly, encountering the soft foreskin covering the head of his cock before resuming her exploration, finding the touch that pleased him. He gasped, thrusting gently into her hand, closing his eyes, as if battling for control.

Touching him was very erotic. Joanna loved putting that look on his face. She wanted more. She wanted to see him lose it completely. Wanted to be the one who made him come. The slave bringing the master to his knees, she thought wickedly.

He groaned and pressed her back against the cushion, angling them so that she could continue to stroke him as he bent down and sucked a hard nipple into his mouth, flicking his tongue against it and making her cry out in return.

Far from being on the edge of losing it, he continued sliding into her grasp, hard as rock with control just as solid. Ben took his time, seducing her further with several long minutes of drugging kisses.

Moving down, he hooked his thumbs into the edges of her lace panties and pulled them off in a clean tug, throwing them out into the room. Leaning back, he took her in and clearly liked what he saw.

His eyes went directly to the back of her hip, settling on her tattoo.

"A tigress…perfect."

She wanted to preen for him. Purr.

Which was not like her at all. Usually, Joanna took control. She didn't play the sex kitten. But with Ben, she didn't mind letting him take over. She didn't want to be the way she was with everyone else, not with him. He shucked his pants, letting her see what she had so far only touched.

He stood, staring at her. "I should tell you something."

She waited, holding her breath and praying for nothing to ruin this.

"I heard you last night," he said, and she didn't understand.

"Heard what?"

"Heard you getting yourself off in the shower. I didn't mean to, but I was taking out garbage and you had your window open."

"Oh," she said, feeling her face burn. "I was thinking about you," she admitted.

"I hoped so. I went back to my room, did the same thing, thinking about you," he confessed, making her minor embarrassment turn into something else altogether. "If you are really my slave, will do you anything I ask?" he said next.

"Happily," she responded, surprised to know she meant it.

"Do it again, so I can see. Touch yourself now," he said, his hand going to his cock even as he told her to do the same. "But don't come."

Her gaze didn't leave his as she lowered her own hand, the sharp sensation brought on by her touch immediately making her cry out and arch off the divan. Her senses went into overdrive from the wait, from watching him watch her.

"Please…I can't hold off," she said, lightening her touch before she exploded.

"Then let me help," he said.

"Oh, yes, please," she said appreciatively, eyeing his achingly erect shaft, and dying to know how he would feel inside her.

"I plan to take my time with you, slave," he said in a soft, gentle way that brought out his Texas drawl and won her over completely.

"Whatever you say," she said, sending him a sultry

look, indulging her inner sex slave as she let her legs fall apart for him, inviting whatever he wanted to do.

She never would have imagined she would enjoy playing the submissive slave, but then again, she had never been with a man she could consider worthy to be her master.

His breathing became a tad rougher. She smiled up at him, beckoning him, feeling more powerful than she imagined a slave would. She enjoyed that, too.

Then his hips were wedged between her thighs, his cock brushing against the wet flesh of her sex and rendering her mute as he kissed his way down her stomach, then lower.

She would have protested the loss of his shaft from its very nice spot between her legs except that he quickly parted her with his hands and replaced the brushing strokes with his lips.

Slow, get-to-know-you strokes at first. Tongue only, lingering and exploratory, as if he were charting her responses, finding out what she liked, what made her writhe, what made her moan.

My master wants to please me, too, she thought in a haze of desire, letting the fantasy take over.

Then his fingers joined in, sliding into her, making her whimper with the need to come, but she was intent on making this heaven last as long as possible.

She lifted up on her elbows to watch, and he looked up, too. Her mind flickered at the sight of him there poised over her, those whiskey eyes hot and aroused as they met hers, his lips and skin slick with her wetness.

The look he gave her was primal, basic, masculine.

Possessive.

He dipped to take her with his mouth again, his eyes

on hers as she watched. This time there was no fighting it, her entire body gave way to him as she spilled over with pleasure. She'd hardly caught her breath when he levered up over her, right where she wanted him to be.

JOANNA EXCITED BEN MORE THAN any woman he could remember. He rubbed his cock along her hot flesh, ramping her arousal back up again, making her ready for him.

"Now, Ben," she demanded, and he paused. He knew she would enjoy being taken hot and hard, maybe even a little rough.

They could do that another time, perhaps.

He wanted them to soak each other up. He wanted to be under her skin. She was already under his. He needed this to be more than a physical connection, which stymied him, but he would think about it more later.

"This is so good," he said softly, covering her, wrapping his hands in silken strands of her dark hair, taking in her face. "I want you," he said against her ear in a slightly threatening tone, feeling her shiver.

"I want you, too," she whispered, arching into him.

"You have the most gorgeous eyes," he said, leaning in to kiss each one. "And a beautiful mouth. Do you know how many times I have thought about the things those lips could do to me?" he said, kissing her long and deep.

She moaned, trying to take him into her body, but he held back. She looped her legs over the backs of his thighs, opening herself more, arching up, pressing against him.

"Hey, remember who's the master here," he said lightly, with a strained chuckle.

He smiled at the frustration that mingled with desire in her eyes. As he slid along the slick space between her thighs, he wasn't sure he could hold out much longer, but he wanted to make sure he had her attention—on his terms—when he took her.

Then she broke him, looking at him fully and simply whispering, "Please, Ben."

"Oh, honey," he said on an expelled breath, wrapping his arms around her and sliding home, sure and deep, as he kissed her. He swallowed the sigh of completion that fell from her lips and groaned again as she wiggled under him to adjust so he was buried even deeper.

Perfect fit, he thought, closing his eyes as her inner muscles hugged his shaft, her strong arms around him as tightly as he was holding her.

Ben moved slowly, rocking his hips back, then forward, nice and slow, drawing it out for them both. A soft cry escaped her lips as she tried to speed him up, but he stayed steady.

Instead, he whispered every single thing he found lovely about her until words started blurring in his mind as pleasure took over. He couldn't stop kissing her, maintaining the steady, slow surging of his body into hers until she tensed, shuddering, warmth flooding their bodies where they were joined, her low moan echoing through him.

Only when he felt her body slacken slightly did he let himself go with a few, short, hard thrusts that launched him over an edge he'd never quite reached before.

It was…powerful.

Their bodies were still connected, wrapped around each other as the passionate haze cleared.

He'd been with a lot of women, but none had ever shaken him to his core the way Joanna did. He couldn't let her see how she affected him. Not now. Not yet. So he took a few deep breaths, cleared his head, got control of himself again before he rose up, looking down into her flushed face.

"Hungry?" he asked, suddenly starving.

JOANNA LAUGHED AT THE unexpected question, but was also thankful for it after the intensity of what had happened between them. She wasn't great with the "afterward" part of sex, usually just heading to the shower, sending her lover on his way or leaving, if she was the one at his place. But this was different, and for one moment after things cleared, she was unsure what was going to happen.

"Yeah, actually. Starving."

It was true, she was suddenly ravenous, and food was the perfect distraction from the messy emotional thoughts that followed her lovemaking with Ben.

Sex, she reminded herself quietly as she rose and grabbed her dress. Not *lovemaking.* Some people used the terms interchangeably, but on a deeper level, she knew they were different. Joanna was very good at one and hadn't had much experience with the other.

Until now, that satisfied, feminine place inside her chided. She ignored it.

"Um, do you mind if I clean up a little while you deal with food?" she asked as he tugged on his jeans. His hair was mussed from her hands, and he looked good enough to eat.

She filed away that thought.

"Sure, the bathroom is at the end of the hall, and I have a few clean shirts on the counter if you want to change into one of them," he said, approaching her and planting a short kiss on her mouth. "Actually, I'm going to run over to the bar for a second, to get some beers, and I'll be right back."

"Sounds good."

Joanna walked toward the bathroom, pausing, waiting until she heard the door shut behind Ben.

This was her chance. Walking quickly to the main room, she made a beeline for the desk, and quickly searched the drawers. She clicked on the laptop, though that required a password.

No time for that. Maybe if she could get in here again, she could grab a USB and try to download what he had and crack it open later, or send it over to Don.

Guilt hovered as she lifted up the blotter, searched for anything that could indicate that Ben was either in trouble or in cahoots with the people after him. She found nothing.

He'd be back in an instant, so she headed for the shower.

In the bathroom, she hit the light and groaned at her own reflection in the mirror, finding it nowhere near as attractive as Ben's mussed look. Her hair was pushed up on the back of her head and stuck to her face—sex hair—and her lips were too red from his kissing. Her eyes were soft, blurry and reflected the satisfaction he had given her. She refocused on towels, washing up and getting her hair back to something that looked normal.

She chose a light flannel shirt folded on the hamper; it was huge, but she rolled up the cuffs and the tails hit her below her butt, providing just enough coverage. As she did so, she noted his running clothes from the night before thrown into the basket by the sink, and her eye landed on what seemed to be a blood stain. Picking the shirt up gingerly, she figured the stain could have come from one of his abrasions, though wouldn't the shirt also be damaged in that spot, then?

Frowning, she bent her head forward, picking up the faintest scent of gunpowder, which made her stomach drop. She should get the stain analyzed, but how could she get his shirt out of the house without him noticing?

Eyeing the window on the other side of the room, she thought about dropping it outside to pick up later, but he'd surely miss it, and she was probably the only other person to be in his bathroom in the past day or so.

Joanna didn't want to believe that Ben could be keeping secrets from her; she didn't think he was in bed with the bad guys, but she wasn't sure how far he'd go to protect himself and the people he cared about. If someone had made a move, had Ben disposed of the threat himself?

"Joanna? You ready to eat?" he called from the hall. She closed her eyes and walked out, shirt in hand, smiling.

"Yeah, sorry. That smells great. How come leftovers always are better than the meal itself?" she asked, arriving in the kitchen to see he had also pulled on a shirt and was busy filling plates with heaps of the Italian food they had ignored at the restaurant.

"There's time for the flavors to set. And good sex makes everything better," he added, looking up at her with so much heat she thought she might wither on the spot. His eyes landed on the shirt in her hand. "What are you doing with that?"

"Oh, I noticed it had a bad stain, probably from where you fell. You shouldn't let it set like that, it'll be permanent. I can take it and get it out for you. Believe me, growing up with two males in the house, I'm an expert in lifting stains, and this is too nice of a shirt to ruin," she commented with a smile, almost ashamed of how easily the lie came.

Ben shrugged, and laughed lightly. "I'd appreciate that, though there's really no need. I can send it out to the cleaners."

"Why spend the money? Let me have it for a few days, and it'll be as good as new."

"Sure," he said casually, triggering her doubts. If he were trying to hide something, would he be so easy to let her take the shirt?

Unable to find a good response, she settled for smiling as she took some plates of bread and butter from him, returning for wine and glasses as he carried plates to the small dining table in the next room.

Ben's home was simple, square and masculine. Everything was constructed of wood, brick and earthenware, and what was painted was done in basic, warm shades.

She liked it.

Antique firearms were on display in a glass case in the small dining room, and she took in the picture in a nice frame on the mantel of a man standing with a young boy, both of them handling a very large fish, obviously taken somewhere near the coast.

"Is that your grandfather and you?" she asked, digging into her food.

"Yeah. He'd head down to Galveston for a fishing trip once a year, and that was the first time he took me, for my thirteenth birthday," Ben said, smiling affectionately at the memory.

"My father and brother would go fishing sometimes," she said with a smile, forgetting herself.

"It doesn't sound like they included you in much," he said sympathetically. "It must have been hard not having your mother."

She took a large bite of her pasta, delaying any response to the question. She wished she hadn't said anything; she didn't want to lie about her family any more. They didn't deserve it, the unflattering portrait she'd painted to go with her cover, and because she didn't want to lie to Ben any more than she had to.

"Well, I never really wanted to go," she said, and at least that was the truth.

She steered the conversation more toward him as they ate, enjoying the stories of boyhood adventures and his grandfather, Cash Callahan, who sounded like a character straight from a Hemingway novel from the way Ben related his grandfather's adventures.

Joanna could tell Ben missed him. She put her hand over his and picked up her wine for a sip.

"You've had your share of adventures, too, I bet. What was it like, being a SEAL?"

"It was everything. My life, who I was. When I was gone, I hardly thought about home, everything was about my team, the missions. I knew I wanted to be a SEAL the minute I saw a documentary on cable when I was a kid. The extreme training, the missions. It was all I cared about until I could get out of high school, even graduated early so I could join up."

"All you cared about? No girlfriends, no sports?" she inquired, really wanting to know.

"I played baseball for a bit, but nothing serious. Any sports I did were to keep training for the military, much to my parents' dismay. Girls, sure. No teenage boy can ignore those."

She smiled at that, and could only imagine him as a teenager. He would have driven girls wild, for sure. "Your parents didn't want you to go?"

"Not really. Granddad started this ranch when he got back from the war, and my dad took it over with Mom when they got married. I guess he thought Granddad, after serving in the war, had built a legacy that was supposed to keep us here on home soil, but I needed to go. At first Dad and Mom really resisted, but Granddad helped them see that it was something they should let me do."

"It sounds like you had a special relationship with him."

"Yeah, which is why I can't quite forgive myself for not being here when he passed," Ben said, raw pain flickering in his expression.

"I'm sure he understood—was proud of you," she offered, feeling that it was hardly enough.

"I know that, but you know, sometimes life just hands us regrets, and there's nothing we can do about it. Just have to carry them along with us, I suppose."

She slid her chair over to sit closer to him. She didn't say anything, lifted his hand to her lips, kissed his fingers. The gesture was meant to be comforting, supportive, but his eyes lit with desire and she felt the answering stir in her own body and didn't resist when he slid his hand into her hair and pulled her in for a wine-saturated kiss.

Passion spiked quickly, which surprised her, given the satisfaction they'd provided for each other only an hour or so ago. As he pulled back from the kiss, Ben's gaze traced her face.

"I don't want you to have any regrets about this," he said, and for the first time, she was tempted just to tell him everything before this all went too far.

But she couldn't. Maybe he would be okay with it—maybe he would accept and understand—but instinct told her that wasn't the case. If he pushed her away, if he told her to leave, more was at stake than her love life. If she left, she would have failed at her job—which wasn't even the most important thing to her, she realized with mild shock.

The more important issue was that she could lose Ben. If someone came after him, if she lost him because she wasn't here, even with all of his skills, that was a regret she wouldn't be able to live with.

For now, she wanted him. Wanted to be with him, wanted to keep him safe.

She moved her hands down to release the buttons of the shirt she wore, enjoying how his gaze followed her actions, his face softening with desire.

"No regrets," she said, and was almost able to convince herself it was true.

7

WITH A LUMP IN HIS THROAT Charlie watched Lisa exit the kitchen's walk-in freezer. He loved her so damned much, it was nearly killing him. She put down the huge pork roast she'd carried out to thaw over the weekend for Monday's pulled pork specials, and beamed a smile at him that made him feel like a million bucks.

And lower than dirt.

"Hey, you okay?" she asked, walking up and putting a soft hand to his face, concerned. She was always more concerned about everyone else than about herself. That's why he had to do anything necessary to protect her.

Risk his life, lie to his friends. Whatever it took.

He turned his face into her palm, planting a kiss there, closing his eyes so that she wouldn't see too much.

He'd find a way out of this mess. He loved her, and he loved the kids. He had to protect them, too. He had a ring. He was going to propose as soon as they were out of this, and then they would be a family.

Buying himself more time, he leaned in and kissed

FREE Merchandise is **'in the Cards'** for you!

Dear Reader,

We're giving away FREE MERCHANDISE!

Seriously, we'd like to reward you for reading this novel by giving you **FREE MERCHANDISE** worth over **$20**. And no purchase is necessary!

You see the Jack of Hearts sticker above? Paste that sticker in the box on the Free Merchandise Voucher inside. Return the Voucher promptly...and we'll send you valuable Free Merchandise!

Thanks again for reading one of our novels—and enjoy your Free Merchandise with our compliments!

Pam Powers

Pam Powers

P.S. Look inside to see what Free Merchandise is **"in the cards"** for you!

The Reader Service - Here's how it works:

Accepting your 2 free books and 2 free mystery gifts (gifts valued at approximately $10.00) places you under no obligation to buy anything. You may keep the books and gifts and return the shipping statement marked "cancel." If you do not cancel, about a month later we'll send you 6 additional books and bill you just $4.49 each in the U.S. or $4.96 each in Canada. That's a savings of at least 14% off the cover price. It's quite a bargain! Shipping and handling is just 50¢ per book in the U.S. and 75¢ per book in Canada.* You may cancel at any time, but if you choose to continue, every month we'll send you 6 more books, which you may either purchase at the discount price or return to us and cancel your subscription.

*Terms and prices subject to change without notice. Prices do not include applicable taxes. Sales tax applicable in N.Y. Canadian residents will be charged applicable taxes. Offer not valid in Quebec. All orders subject to credit approval. Books received may not be as shown. Credit or debit balances in a customer's account(s) may be offset by any other outstanding balance owed by or to the customer. Please allow 4 to 6 weeks for delivery. Offer available while quantities last.

If offer card is missing write to: The Reader Service, P.O. Box 1867, Buffalo, NY 14240-1867 or visit www.ReaderService.com

BUSINESS REPLY MAIL

FIRST-CLASS MAIL PERMIT NO. 717 BUFFALO, NY

POSTAGE WILL BE PAID BY ADDRESSEE

THE READER SERVICE
PO BOX 1867
BUFFALO NY 14240-9952

NO POSTAGE NECESSARY IF MAILED IN THE UNITED STATES

her soft and long, but also because he needed to remind himself what he was fighting for.

He'd been tempted to tell Ben that he knew, but that would only make things worse. Ben would insist on telling the Feds, and Charlie couldn't risk that. He had to deal with this on his own.

Pulling back, he studied Lisa's sweet face and kissed her on the nose, smiling.

"I'm fine. Just distracted, thinking about you wearing that dress I bought you for the party tomorrow," he said, playing along. He could never let her suspect what danger she and her kids were in.

Because of him.

"I thought you might have been more distracted by the idea of taking it off," she said with a wink.

He groaned, gathering her in close. "Now you've done it," he teased back, pushing his worries away. "I won't be able to think about anything else now."

She pulled back, planting a sweet kiss on his mouth. "Good. Now I'd better get two more of those roasts out. One will never be enough for the Monday crowd."

Reluctantly, he let her go, whistling appreciatively and making her giggle as she walked away from him with a little shimmy. He walked out back for a minute to get some air, and noticed Ben's parked car and the lights on low in his front room.

He'd thought his friend would have been over at the ranch tonight, helping get the party organized, but maybe Ben had decided to turn in early.

Ben had always been the better man. A real, honest-to-goodness hero. Charlie's armor was a bit tarnished, but Lisa made him feel all shiny. Like a real man, not one who had secretly had a drug problem for the better part of a year as he recovered from his surgery just three years before. It seemed like a long time ago.

War had been hell, and coming home had been harder. He took the loss of his leg as well as he could, though the pain was overwhelming at times, the physical therapy excruciating, as he learned to use his prosthesis. Worse had been the worry that he'd never be a complete man again. Never have a complete life. Military duty had been the only time he'd ever really belonged somewhere, and losing that had hit him hard.

They'd stepped him down off the pain meds and anti-depressants in the hospital, but he'd only lasted a few weeks on his own. It had been easy enough to find the same stuff, better even, on the street.

When Ben had come to his apartment in Houston to offer him a job, a purpose, he'd been higher than a kite. Ben had noticed that Charlie was using, of course, and Charlie had concocted a story about mistakenly mixing up his prescriptions, which Ben had accepted easily enough.

Charlie had always tried to live up to his friend's standards, to be like him, but he had never quite made it. He loved Ben, and he resented him. Everything always seemed to come so easily for Ben Callahan, but this was one time when maybe Charlie could come out on top for a change.

Charlie had assured him the drugs were prescription and that he would be off them soon. It was the last lie he'd told his best friend until now.

Charlie had stopped taking the drugs as soon as he'd stepped foot into the Lucky Break, knowing Ben would kick him right back out the door if he suspected he had a habit. So he'd worked hard to put it all behind him. Prove himself.

And then there was Lisa. He'd thought she was his reward for fighting his way back, for doing the right thing.

Until Joe had come around a few weeks back. Joe was Charlie's former street supplier. Charlie had told him to get lost until Joe arrived at the house, beaten pretty badly. The men who were after Ben had discovered Charlie's past, and used Joe to make contact. They threatened to tell Lisa about his drug habit, and, perhaps, hurt her—or the kids—if Charlie didn't find a way to make Ben refuse to testify. Or he could kill Ben—they didn't care which. They'd laughed at him, saying that at least they'd given him a choice. Apparently though, Charlie wasn't moving fast enough, and they were getting antsy. It was why they'd sent the goon to the bar and to Lisa's house—to remind him.

But Charlie's hands were tied. He knew there was no way to get Ben not to testify. He wasn't a guy who would stand down.

Charlie certainly didn't intend to kill him, either.

Killing *himself* had crossed his mind, but that wouldn't stop these guys from coming after Ben or Lisa. He couldn't stand to think of losing everything he had. Ben would want nothing to do with him, and neither would Lisa, once they found out. Time was getting short. It was only a couple of weeks until the trial, and Charlie's time was running out. The guy who'd come to the bar had made that clear.

He would find a way out of it, he thought, taking a second glance at the lights in Ben's windows before opening the door to the bar, hoping Lisa was almost done with her weekend prep.

If he could find a way to get Ben to change his mind, and no one would get hurt, then he could be the hero for a change, and he could ask Lisa to marry him. No one would be the wiser, but Charlie would know he'd saved them.

He just had to figure out how. Joining Lisa near the door, he caught her smile and knew he would find a way out of this that would keep them all safe.

He had to.

"WOW, IT'S PACKED," JOANNA said as she found a spot on the side of the unpaved road that led to the main house of the Double C Ranch. The place was named for Ben's grandfather, Cash Callahan. Today, it was the site of Ben's father's birthday party. "I guess Ben wasn't kidding when he said this wasn't a small family gathering."

Hank and Rachel Callahan—Ben's parents—were the second generation to work this ranch, Joanna knew from the profile report she'd memorized, and Ben was now the third.

"Everyone loves Hank and Rachel's parties," Lisa said with a grin. Her car had died, and Joanna had offered to pick her and her two kids up for the party. Ben was okay with it, as he had taken off early to help his parents get things ready, though she wondered how he would have the energy. Neither of them had gotten much sleep. She'd caught a few hours after he left, and then had managed to get back to her apartment unseen, fortunately, as the bar was closed for the day.

She was anxious to see him again, and she wasn't. Sex always changed things, except it hadn't been only sex. They'd talked, shared and done things she didn't usually do. Including falling asleep in his bed. There was something about sleeping with someone—sharing a bed—that was more intimate than having sex with them.

He'd made her feel everything straight down to her bones. After she'd seduced him right there in his dining room, they'd finally made it to his bed, and under the warm blankets it was as though everything tense or worried inside of her had evaporated.

She'd felt safe.

She was happy finally to be here at the party; it made her nervous to have Ben out of her sight for long periods of time, out of her protection. At least that's what she told herself.

Taking in the dozens of cars and trucks parked along the roadside and several other people arriving on horseback, she was even more glad that she'd come. It was the weekend, which meant time off from the bar anyway. Her duty to watch out for Ben didn't go away, but she was looking forward to this down time. Certainly no one would try anything in a large group of the Callahans' friends—most of them Texans with guns. Monday would be soon enough for dealing with reality.

Joanna relaxed and checked on the kids in the back seat in the rearview mirror. Abe and Patsy sat quietly playing with some handheld game that had had them transfixed for the entire ride. Not a peep. Abe was seven and Patsy was four. They were polite, good kids, and Joanna, who hadn't spent much time with children, found them agreeable to be around.

As soon as they were parked, Abe and Patsy morphed into banshees. They squealed with excitement as seatbelt straps were released, and they ran from the car as if it were on fire, launching themselves into the backyard crowd.

"They're excited," Joanna commented with a grin, watching them run.

"The Callahans always have special things set up for the kids. I haven't had much chance to do things with them lately, I've been working so much. I hope that can change once I have my divorce settled, and now that we have you at the bar," Lisa said, sighing.

Joanna nodded, guilt assaulting her. What could she say? *Sorry, but this is just a temporary thing, and in a few weeks you'll likely never see me again.*

Her gun was in her bag at her side, which grounded her somewhat, but this was a party, and she wanted to enjoy it. She looked down at her white sandals, also Lisa's, as grass tickled her newly painted toes, when her cell phone rang.

"You go ahead, I need to take this," she said to Lisa.

"I can wait—take your time," Lisa said with a smile, but Joanna could see the curiosity light in her eyes.

Answering the phone, she turned away and lowered her voice.

"Hi, Don. What's up?"

"We have a report back on the stain on that shirt—it's not Callahan's, but nothing popped in the DNA database, and so it's a dead end, except that it's not his."

"Anything with the gunpowder residue?"

"Only faint traces. Could have been from his own gun, if he was out shooting recently."

Joanna nodded. "He does have a range out back. I'll try to get a copy of his hard drive and emails, and maybe we'll find something there."

"Hold off on that. It's risky—at this point, all we have is a guy with a bloodstain on his shirt, and there could be a hundred explanations for that. Did you ask him about it?"

She thought back to the moment when she was standing mostly naked in Ben's house after making love, and shook her head.

"It wasn't the right moment."

"Well, back down for now, unless you have a stronger reason to suspect he's in trouble," Don said.

"Okay. That's all?"

"Yeah. Have a good weekend, Jo."

He hung up, leaving her wondering if she was imagining trouble where there wasn't any. Maybe because she was lying to everyone around her right now, she just assumed they were lying to her, too.

"Ben is going to pass out when he sees you in that dress," Lisa continued, "I've always loved it, even though I am a tad too short to wear it well. But on you…it's perfect." The soft yellow dress, one of Lisa's that Joanna had borrowed, had a sweetheart bodice and full skirt. Not her usual fare—not by a long shot. At first, it made her uncomfortable, feeling overly feminine, but then she'd decided to wear it because it was so different from what she usually wore. Sometimes different was good.

"Thanks. Yours is gorgeous, too. It's kind of nice to be out of my bar clothes," she said.

"Thank you. Charlie bought this for me for my birthday. He saw me admiring it in a shop window, and went back to get it. It's the most thoughtful gift I ever received," Lisa said, sounding misty.

Joanna diverted the conversation before she had to

deal with tears, even happy ones, something she definitely wasn't comfortable with.

"I doubt Callahan will even notice," she murmured as they walked closer to the house.

"Why did you call him by his last name?"

Because it's how they always referred to him back at headquarters, Joanna thought, but couldn't say that, of course. Actually, it had been a slip.

"I don't know. Because he's the boss, I suppose. It's less familiar."

"Huh. At this point, I think you're getting pretty 'familiar,' if what I saw when I caught you two walking over to his place last night is any indication," Lisa teased. "From the size of that doggie bag, seemed like you didn't even wait for dinner."

Joanna stuttered, unsure what to say, not wanting to lie to this woman any more than she already had, but also unsure how much to reveal. As she fought the indecision, Lisa let out a whoop that drew attention from a few of the other people in the front yard, and smiled widely.

"About time someone got under that man's skin. He needs it more than I can say. I had a feeling about you two," she said, smiling smugly.

"Well, don't get too excited. It was just a …slip. I'm sure it won't happen again," Joanna said. "And please don't tell anyone else, even Charlie, okay? I don't want Ben thinking I told everyone."

Lisa nodded. "Sure thing, hon. Take my advice, though, don't get involved in any poker games tonight," Lisa said with another chuckle as they started heading toward the backyard again.

Joanna hated that she had been read so easily, and

that Lisa thought she couldn't hold her own in a poker game. They wouldn't even let her in on the games back at headquarters, where she'd cleaned too many of the guys out.

But she apparently wasn't as good at this new game.

"Lisa, I can't afford to lose this job, and while Ben is great, I'm worried about what he'd think if people found out."

Lisa sighed. "I wouldn't worry about that. Ben is a good man, Joanna. The kind that doesn't come along often. And at least you won't be wanting for a hat today."

"What?" Joanna asked, confused.

"It's kind of a tradition at this party. If a woman comes to an event without a hat, she's intending to try to get one of the cowboys at the party to give her his, or she's available for them to offer it."

"Why?" Joanna peered up at the bright sky, squinting. It was hot, but there was plenty of shade and a light breeze. She had a hat, but it didn't quite go with the dress so she had skipped it.

"It's a way to let someone know you're interested, to pair up for the evening, or maybe even longer. You'll notice the only women here wearing their own hats are married or spoken for."

"So if a guy gives me his hat, that means I'm their date for the party?"

"More or less, yes. Or you can try to steal it, which usually means, if he's agreeable, that you and he might have a little fun after the party, too."

Joanna knew that cowboys and their hats—and marshals and their hats, for that matter—had a long history with a lot of symbolic meaning. She knew hats could indicate everything from personal taste to income bracket to political leanings in some parts of the country, but mostly they were used to keep the sun or the rain off your head.

This was a new twist she hadn't counted on and wasn't sure what to do with.

They turned the corner of the big house into the yard where most of the partygoers congregated, and just as Joanna was about to reply to Lisa, her eyes locked on to Ben's and she forgot what she was going to say.

Words were lost as she remembered that the last time she'd looked into those caramel eyes, he'd been deep, deep inside her.

"Yep, definitely stay away from the poker tables," Lisa said humorously, patting her on the arm. "I'm gonna go find the kids and Charlie, and steal that man's hat."

Joanna looked back to where Ben had been standing, but he was gone.

"Well, aren't you a picture," someone said from behind her, a voice she didn't recognize, and she turned to find a nice-looking cowboy smiling in her direction, holding two glasses of something cold. "But kind of a sad one, standing here all alone," he said, handing her one of the drinks.

Joanna paused before accepting. As the guy handed her the drink, he pulled his well-worn dress hat off and placed it to his chest with a slight nod.

"I'm Andrew Meyers," he said pleasantly, looking at her with a pair of sparking blue eyes that danced beneath a downright rakish lock of black hair falling forward on his forehead.

Joanna smiled as he replaced his hat. He was a bit

young for her, but charming, and she had no doubt that he was used to bowling women his own age over with that smile.

"Joanna," she said, being friendly—but not too friendly—and offering a nod back.

"Beautiful name. Are you new here? I don't remember seeing you around."

Joanna briefly filled in that she was a new Lucky Break employee, and they made casual chitchat for a while, though she wondered where Ben had gone. Was he avoiding her?

Andy, as a lot of young guys tend to do, started talking way too much about himself, and she smiled, nodded and finished her drink while planning a quick escape at the first available moment. She panicked as he took off his hat, and appeared to be asking her if she would like to take it.

She was rescued before she had to deal with an awkward refusal.

"Andy, I think Jill is looking for you," a familiar voice said from behind Joanna, and she turned to see Ben approaching them.

Joanna quirked an eyebrow at Andy, trying not to smile. "Jill?"

"Girl I came with," he said, smiling widely. "It's not serious, though." He had the audacity to wink at her before he tipped his hat again and turned to leave.

"Thanks, Callahan," Andy added sarcastically.

"As if you stood a chance, anyway," Ben joked back, laughing as the younger man went in search of his date.

"He's a piece of work," Joanna said with a chuckle. "Nice guy, but kinda full of himself."

"He is a good kid, but he doesn't get shot down much."

Joanna peered at Ben teasingly, glad they had something to break the ice, someone else to talk about. "Were you worried I would fall victim to his rakish charm?"

"Hardly. I was more worried he would talk you to death," Callahan joked. "And I didn't want you accepting his hat without knowing the story on that."

She laughed. "Don't worry. Lisa filled me in on the whole hat thing."

"Did she now?" he asked, tilting his head and standing a half step closer.

"Yep. If I take one, it means I want to hook up with that guy. If a guy gives it to me, it means I'm his date for the party, and maybe we can hook up later."

"I see you have the basics down," he said in a low tone, his eyes dancing as he lifted his hat from his head and put it on hers. "I'm glad you made it," he added, his tone much warmer.

Joanna cleared her throat, trying to sound casual. His hat was a little big, but he tilted it back so that it was comfortable on her head. It probably looked ridiculous with her dress, but she didn't care.

"Thanks for asking me. I haven't been to a party in a while. Not such a nice one, certainly."

He didn't respond as his eyes drifted over her dress, which would have made her feel self-conscious if she hadn't been equally wowed by his appearance in dress clothes.

He looked good enough to eat, as far as she was concerned, in the worn jeans and T-shirt he often wore at the bar—or in nothing at all. She would have thought that for a girl growing up in Texas with two older males in the house, a cowboy hat wouldn't do a thing, but, wrong again.

His white dress shirt hugged his arms, and, set off with a simple crossover tie, accentuated the broadness of his chest; topped off with the tan felt Stetson, he was handsome times ten. He was still wearing jeans—but nice ones—and dress boots. He looked cool as a cucumber in the afternoon heat. Seeing him in his Sunday cowboy gear, hat and all, had gotten to her.

"That dress is beautiful on you. I'm surprised half the guys here didn't try to pile hats on you," he said, his tone low. "Though I'd have to hurt them if they did."

"Thanks. You clean up pretty nicely yourself," she said, meaning it, and then she took the opportunity that presented itself. "Speaking of clothes, I kind of ruined that shirt I tried to clean for you—I should probably just buy you a new one. Sorry about that," she said, looking up at him from under her lashes.

"Not necessary. It's no big deal, and was nice of you to try."

"How did you end up staining it anyway? I noticed you didn't have any cuts where it was ruined."

Ben looked at her closely. "Why are you so interested?"

"Concerned. I care about you, and—"

Her words seemed to stop them both in their tracks. She knew she meant it—she did care about him—and suddenly felt cheap using that to get him to tell her something she wanted to know.

"It was no big deal. When I was on my way out for my run, I broke up a fight between two guys out back, and one of the guys had been hit in the face. When I helped him to his car, I guess he got that on my shirt is all."

"Oh," she said, smiling. "I feel stupid."

"No need. I like that you were bothered enough to ask. I know after you've been with someone, um, less than trustworthy, things can make you wonder."

"Like bloodstained shirts."

"Yeah. Never be afraid to ask me anything like that up front. I should have told you anyway, but it didn't seem important."

They didn't say anything again for several long moments, and Joanna could feel the heat building again, and not from the sun beating down. Don was right; she had immediately jumped to conclusions, and there had been an explanation after all.

"Your glass is empty. Let me get another lemonade for you," Ben said in a very gentlemanly way.

"That would be nice," she said, smiling at him from under the wide brim of his hat.

Rather than walking away he placed his hands on her shoulders, looking at her closely. The touch of his skin to hers made her close her eyes and wish more than anything that she could just be a regular woman, here to meet a guy at an afternoon picnic. But she wasn't.

Kids' happy screams and laughter echoed across the yard from where they were enjoying a bounce house and other fun activities. Joanna pushed back a strand of hair that kept escaping the braid that Lisa had woven for her.

It all faded to background as Ben's lips touched hers, softly at first and then more insistently, parting them and rubbing the tip of his tongue along them in a very erotic way. He didn't pull her closer or deepen the kiss, but just kept tasting her until she put a hand to his shoulder, leaning back against the fence rail she stood beside, seeking more support.

He stopped, the breath he exhaled a little shaky, as well.

"I'll go get that drink."

"Maybe throw a splash of something stronger in there."

"I'll make it two, then," he said with a wink, and walked away, allowing her the most wonderful view as he did.

Watching the kids play, the people standing around, smiling, talking, she couldn't help but enjoy the moment. To enjoy Ben and the party. He was back in a few minutes carrying two large, icy glasses of lemonade. When she took a sip, she looked up with a laugh.

"Wow…what's in this?"

"Just a splash of some really good tequila."

"It's delicious," she said, taking another sip.

"I have to admit, all I want to do is get you somewhere alone and peel off that dress," he said over the top of his glass, eyes hot.

"I—" She started to say something, though she had no idea what it was. He made her mind go blank when he looked at her like that.

"But I suppose we should join the party," he said with a wicked grin. He took her hand, leading her over to the crowded backyard where a band was playing and tables of food were lined up with enough goodies to feed an army. The air was sweet and smoky with the aroma of barbecue drifting from the black pits behind the tables. Several men manned the grills with beers in one hand and forks and spatulas in the other.

Ben led her into the middle of it all, and within seconds, half the yard was dancing around them, preventing any more conversation.

Ben took her drink and deposited it with his on a nearby table, coming back to pull her up next to him. Joanna stiffened for a second, and he looked down at her.

"Don't like to dance?"

She firmed her jaw, biting her lip. "Never really have had much chance, and I don't think I'm very good at it. Maybe we should—"

"Just hang on, you'll be fine," he said, pulling her in and wrapping one of her hands in his, the other arm loosely around her back. There wasn't anything overtly sexual or suggestive in his movements, but being so close sure made her think sexual and suggestive thoughts.

Lots of them. So many she completely forgot she was dancing, an activity she rarely took part in.

While she'd not been oblivious to the fact that many interested gazes followed them—and a lot of jealous ones, too—no one seemed to notice that she had no idea what she was doing on a dance floor.

Ben's body moved easily next to hers, his hard muscular form seeming to burn right through the thin fabric of her dress even though they were barely touching. She'd hardly noticed that he'd danced them to a less-occupied part of the yard, behind a huge flowering bush that took over one entire side of his parent's large deck.

"We might have a problem," he said, looking down at her, his expression very serious.

"What?" She looked around, alarmed, her hand moving to her thigh reflexively, until she remembered she had put the gun in her bag, which Lisa had insisted on putting away upstairs in the house with hers. Joanna hadn't liked it, but she could hardly argue.

"I can't seem to stop touching you," he said, sliding his hands to her back. "This dress is driving me crazy," he admitted in a voice so thick with desire it was unmistakable.

"That could be a problem, yes," she agreed with a smile.

Ben's hands framed her face and he bent to kiss her when the sound of laughing nearby broke them out of the spell and she saw two kids, probably around ten, spying on them from behind a tree. The pair laughed again as they ducked out of sight.

"I think we've been made," Joanna said dryly, but she was secretly relieved for the interruption. She didn't trust herself with Ben, and certainly didn't need to be seen making out with him in public. In the middle of his parents' yard, no less.

"I think you're right," he said, laughing.

He scrutinized the young spies, and with speed that made her jump, took off after them with a whoop. More peals of laughter filled the air as the interlopers ran away, Ben in pursuit. He quickly caught up with them, assisted by a couple of his cowboy friends, and the kids were screaming in helpless hysterics as the men carried them to the jumping tent and swung them one-two-three into the padded room.

Joanna grinned and settled back against the rail fence to watch as kids raced by, all wanting to be the next one caught and tossed.

Ben would be great with kids, that was clear. She wondered if he wanted his own.

"Sheesh," she said to herself, straightening up and not liking how easily *that* thought had drifted into her brain, nor the warm fuzzy feeling that had come with it.

Having ticked past thirty the year before, she still had time for all of that. The guys she worked with had families, regular lives, but then again, being a parent didn't put them out of the field for almost a year.

She'd spent almost a decade proving herself, building her career, her reputation. She had no illusions about how quickly it would all go down the drain if she let herself get distracted by her biological clock. Even if she never had a child of her own, she could adopt some day if she wanted to—she knew the system was full of kids who needed homes.

There was no rush even to think about it, she told herself, watching Ben throw another squealing kid into the funhouse.

She redirected her thoughts, though it took considerable discipline.

It was the effect of the day. And the man. Being here, amid all of these other families, the kids, the relaxed atmosphere, it was hard not to think about life outside the Marshal Service. Having spent a few weeks with her newly married brother and Lacey—who were also thinking about a family—didn't help matters any.

She'd always thought she was fine on her own, and had no desire for anything more than to do her job well, but now, there was Ben....

He made his way back to her and stood a few feet away, still grinning, and holding his hand out to her.

"The afternoon games are starting. I could use a

partner," he said, eyeing her from head to toe. "Up for the three-legged race?" he asked.

She welcomed the shift in the mood between them, the lighter spirit. Stepping forward, she took his hand and smiled. "Games, huh? So whose butts are we going to kick?"

He laughed, planting a quick kiss on her cheek.

"That's the spirit."

Her second thoughts followed her as they crossed the yard back to a large field where people were gathering, obviously getting ready for some events. His touch, his large hand around hers, thrilled her far more than it should, but she didn't back away. His touch made her want him more than it should. Everything with Ben was more than it should be.

Before she could think too much about it, he was tying a rope to her right ankle and she looked down as he slid his other hand down the back of her opposite thigh, igniting sparks everywhere. She held her breath, relieved she had decided to stow her holstered gun here.

"Ready for me to tie you up?" he asked, wiggling his eyebrows.

Chuckling out loud, she nodded, abandoning her doubts in the face of his silly sexiness.

"Let's go for it." Even as she said the words, she wondered if she was talking about the race or something else. Her worries were soon lost in the frantic race, and Joanna did something she hadn't done in a very long time.

She had fun.

8

THEY COMPETED IN SEVERAL rounds of a three-legged-race championship—in which Ben and Joanna came in second only because he'd tripped while trying to catch a peek down her dress. Then there was a round of Capture the Flag and a water-balloon fight the kids started when they ambushed the adults. Now, Ben sat nursing a beer and cooling down. He was particularly enjoying the view as Joanna stretched out beside him on the soft grass.

She had a smudge of dirt on her cheek and grass stains on her pretty dress. She didn't seem to care, which didn't surprise him at all. She had a fiercely competitive spirit, balanced by a fun-loving nature that had her pushing hard to win and dissolving in laughter when they didn't.

She might be new to shooting guns, but was dead aim with a water balloon, as his soaked clothing proved. He'd gotten his own shots in, as had the kids. All in all, it was fun—and exhausting.

They'd come to sit in the sun to dry off, but the shade had taken over as afternoon shadows started to stretch long over the yard. He didn't want to move from the spot, enjoying just being here with Joanna.

He looked down, taking in the long, tan length of her legs, sandals long abandoned, feet crossed at the ankles. The peach-colored paint on her toes intrigued him, as she didn't seem to do those kinds of girly things too often.

He hoped it was for his benefit.

Her dress still covered her adequately, but had ridden up on her thighs a little, garnering his interest.

Slim hips and a small waist narrowed up to her top where the dress gapped slightly, providing him the peek he had been after earlier. He liked her shape, and the smooth, womanly strength she exuded, the easy way she moved.

He particularly liked the way she wrapped herself around him, took him whole, made him feel as though he could sink into her until the entire world went away.

Taking in her face, her eyes closed, lips parted, he reached out, drawing his finger along the side of her cheek.

Her eyes opened, meeting his. They weren't alone, others were milling around, seeking out some dinner before an evening of dancing started, but they were alone enough.

"Hey."

"Hey," she said back.

"Did I wake you up?"

"Was I snoring?" she asked, not seeming at all embarrassed by the possibility.

"Nope."

"Then no, not sleeping," she said with a smile, looking up at him peacefully.

"You do saw some wood, though, I'll hand you that," he said, teasing.

She laughed. "Yeah, I know. My brother taped me once to convince me it was true."

He laughed. It was nice that she had some good memories of growing up.

"This place is perfect," she said, pushing up to her elbows, staring at the main house. "Growing up here with your family, your parents…it's like a fairy tale."

"Well, maybe not like that. Ranches are hard work, and we went through some tough times, financially and otherwise, but yeah, it was nice growing up here."

"And only you? No brothers or sisters?"

"Mom and Dad tried, but Mom had some condition that made it hard for her to carry to term after me, so they settled for what they got," he said with a sideways smile. "And we had Charlie. He pretty much lived here, too, since his family was such a mess. He was more like a brother, really, than a friend."

"That's nice that you all would take him in like that," she said, rolling over and propping on her elbows, very aware, he knew, from the gleam in her eyes of the peek she was allowing him now.

Ben found it suddenly very difficult to track the conversation and couldn't care less about talking about his childhood.

"Come here, I want to show you something."

"Sounds promising," she said, and stood, following him down behind the barns and through some brush, the sounds of the party fading behind them. Under the late afternoon sky that was quickly fading to sunset, a few stars were winking. When he stopped, they were standing in front of a small pond surrounded by rocks.

"The springs that feeds up into this land. One of the reasons my grandfather settled here is that the water runs under several acres of the ranch," he said, reaching behind her to pull the zipper of her dress down.

She simply stood before him as he gently lowered the dress from her shoulders and laid it over a tree branch close by. It took him seconds to get out of his own clothes, and she stripped off her underwear as well, understanding.

Without saying a word, he held his hand out to her, and she took it, both of them running into the water.

Joanna gasped and let out a squeal as her fingers dug into his shoulders.

"This is freezing!" she exclaimed breathlessly.

"Just for the first minute or so until you get used to it. Here, I can help you warm up," he said, bringing her naked form close to his.

It had been hours since he'd kissed her, and he couldn't wait another minute, finding her mouth as her arms and legs went around him. His hands slid down to hold her backside as he kept them steady in the water.

"What if someone comes over here?" she asked, nibbling at his throat.

"They won't. Most people don't even know it's here," he said confidently.

"Well, how nice for us."

"Yeah, I thought so," he agreed. Leaning down under the cool surface of the water he sucked a hard nipple into his mouth, drawing on her until she was crying out and he had to come up for air.

"Oh, that's so nice, with the water," she said breathlessly.

"I'm a SEAL," he responded with a grin. "Water is where I'm best."

He shifted them slightly, and slipped inside her, the contrast between the heat of her body and the cold water making him groan aloud as well.

They stopped talking as their bodies fused, his hands grinding her against him in a rhythm that soon brought both of them to the edge.

"Joanna, hold your breath."

"Why? I don't think—"

"Don't worry, I've got you. Relax and take three deep breaths with me, exhaling completely, and on the third one, exhale completely but hold it, okay? If you can't hold it once we're under, just let go of me and we'll come right back to the surface. It's just inches away. Do you trust me?"

A pause, and his heart slammed as his body pushed him forward for completion, but he waited.

"Okay," she said on a hushed breath. "But shouldn't I inhale to hold my breath?"

"Exhaling is the trick, believe me."

"To what?"

"You'll see," he promised.

"Okay."

"One," he said, sucking in a deep breath and releasing it with her, at the same time filling her and withdrawing.

"Two," he said against her cheek, doing the same, and feeling her start to tighten around him.

"Three." They both exhaled deeply as he took them under water, holding her to him and pumping into her fast and hard until he felt her spasm against him, her fingers digging in as his own mind-bending orgasm exploded from his body.

Breaking the surface, they both gasped for air and sought each other again. She grabbed on to him tightly, still shaking.

"Are you okay?" he asked, worried that maybe his plan had not gone as he'd hoped. He thought she had enjoyed it, but—

"Okay? Who needs air?" she said, her voice trembling as she wound herself around him. "And I don't want to stop," she said, biting his shoulder.

He wouldn't have thought it possible after the climax he'd just had, but she made him hard again within seconds and took him inside one more time.

After another mind-bending release under the water, Ben's legs were shaking, too, as they made it to the edge of the spring where he collapsed with her beside him. They caught their breath on the sand, where the lingering warmth and a breeze dried the water from their skin in minutes.

"So where did you learn that little trick?" she asked, rolling over, one arm splayed over his chest.

"You've heard of autoerotic asphyxiation?"

She nodded. "Dangerous stuff. People die."

"Yeah, and it's doubly stupid because they're missing the point anyway. It's not inhaling and holding your breath that makes it stronger, more intense, it's the exhale. You need to take the deep breaths in and out, and exhaling pushes the thoracic diaphragm lower, increasing contractions. Being in the water isn't necessary, but I had a feeling it would be nice, all of our senses deprived except for focusing on the pleasure," he explained.

"You learn that in the SEALs?"

He laughed. "I can't divulge the source of my intel," he said, though the truth was that he had learned the breathing trick from a yoga instructor he'd dated for a while.

"We should probably get dressed and back to the party before anyone misses us," he said, kissing her before he stood up.

"Okay. Thanks for inviting me today, and for showing me this place," she said, sounding almost wistful, as if she were a little sad.

"I wanted you here with me," he said, pulling on his shirt and watching her dress under the moonlight, his heart stuttering in his chest. "This isn't just sex for me, Joanna. You should know that."

It was true, and he figured he might as well say it now.

She pushed her fingers through her hair, quiet for a moment in a way that made his heart sink.

"I know. Me, too," she said, almost too quietly for him to hear her, but he did.

He couldn't blame her for being apprehensive. It had only been a few days, and it was so intense he was out of his depth. But something told him that she was different from any other woman he'd ever known.

"We have time. No pressure, okay?" he said, tugging her into an embrace.

She didn't say anything, but nodded against his chest. He could feel the tension that had returned to her frame, and hugged her closer. Whatever doubts she had, he was intent on erasing them and making this work.

Whatever was between them, he knew it was something special, and he wasn't about to let it go.

TWO HOURS LATER, BEN THREW THE last dishrag down the laundry chute that went from the kitchen to the basement and leaned back against the counter in exhaustion.

His mother, Rachel, smiled at him, tired but happy as she pushed up on her toes to kiss his cheek.

"Thanks for the help with the clean-up, Ben. And Joanna, too. She didn't have to do that."

Through the large kitchen window Ben heard Joanna's laugh filter in from the backyard where she had been helping his dad clean up. Lisa had left with Charlie, and Jo had just pitched in. Of course she had, he thought with a smile.

"This one's different," his mother said, watching him with a sly look.

"Yes, she is." He wanted to play it cool, but he couldn't seem to wipe the stupid smile from his face.

"Your father had that same look on his face when he used to look at me—and I'd say she feels the same way, if I'm any judge."

"We're taking it one day at a time."

"Smart. But I like her, too, at least what I know of her."

"It was a great party," he said, changing the subject as he heard his father's booming voice approaching the house, the back door opening.

"One of our best," his father agreed as he walked in.

"Always did have ears like a hawk," Ben answered, grinning at his father, who deposited a box of unused paper plates, cups and other items on the counter, followed by Joanna, who hefted a similar box.

Ben stepped forward. "Hey, let me take that," he said, reaching to take the box from Joanna, who made a raspberry-like noise and carried the large carton to the counter herself.

"I have it. Relax," she said.

Ben didn't miss the amused, knowing look his parents shared, but he chose to ignore it.

"She's no slouch, this one," Hank, his father, said, grinning at Joanna with clear admiration.

If Ben weren't sure that his father was two-hundred-percent in love with and devoted to his mother, he'd think Hank had a crush.

"I enjoyed lending a hand," Joanna said, clearly a fan of the senior Callahan as well. "It was a wonderful day. I haven't been to a party like that in well…ever."

"Hank can never do anything small," Rachel said, her eyes twinkling at her husband.

Ben watched Joanna watching them, and then she looked away. He saw it in her eyes, the distance. Her upbringing had been a lot different than his, with her mom taking off, her dad gone, and her brother not caring much. Standing here in the kitchen of the house he'd grown up in, with both of his parents, he wished he could somehow erase any of the past pain she'd suffered.

His father cleared his throat as Ben realized the kitchen had gone quiet, and he'd been caught staring at Joanna for a minute too long.

"Long day," Ben agreed, clearing his throat. "We should probably head back to the bar." He checked the clock. It was well after midnight.

"Nonsense, you'll both stay here. It's too late to drive home and we have more than enough room upstairs."

"Oh, I couldn't impose," Joanna broke into the conversation.

"I won't hear of you driving back home tonight. After all of this work you helped us with, you get a good night's sleep and we'll have a nice breakfast. The bar is closed tomorrow, right, Ben?"

"Yep. Sunday is our day of rest," he said, smiling at Joanna.

Cornered. That's how she looked, but maybe only to him. He wondered why. What had made her so skittish?

"I—I don't have any change of clothes with me," she said.

"No problem, Joanna," his mom said, taking her by the arm. I have plenty of extras upstairs, and I think a few of my things from my younger years will fit you. I'll show you the shower, and you can have the guest room on the end, it's the one with the best view in the morning," his mother chirped.

Ben shook his head, smiling, knowing Joanna didn't stand a chance. He also knew the room she was taking Joanna to didn't have that great a view, but it was right next to his—on the opposite side of the house from his parents' master bedroom.

His mom really wanted grandchildren, but Ben wasn't willing to think that far ahead just yet.

"That's one heck of a woman, son," his father said as the two women left. "But she's no waitress."

Ben cocked an eyebrow at his dad, who seemed more tired than usual.

"You okay, Dad?"

"Yes, I'm fine. Just a long day. Don't change the subject."

"I don't know what you mean," Ben said. "Of course she's a waitress."

"She has a different way about her. Strong, doesn't ask for help and isn't slow to offer it," Hank explained.

"She's a waitress, she's on her feet lifting heavy trays all day, serving people," Ben said, shrugging.

"True, though that doesn't explain the way she scans the area when she thinks you aren't looking, or…I don't know. There's just an air about her."

Ben knew what his dad meant—he'd noticed too, when they were shooting, for instance.

"She had a tough time growing up—and more recently, too," Ben went on, telling his father about Joanna's ex, and some of her other troubles. He didn't want to betray her confidence, but he knew what he said was safe with his dad.

"Hard to think of that lovely young woman having all that hardship. But now she has you," his father said confidently.

"It's not like that, Dad. Not yet, anyway," Ben said nervously, starting to feel as if his parents were counting on something he didn't even know was real just yet.

"Of course it is. I'm old, not stupid. Whatever needs working out, you two will do it. She's holding on to something—something you need to know about, take my word for it. But you'll work it out, because she's the one. I would put money on it," his father said.

They said goodnight, and Ben walked down to his room, pausing by the upstairs bathroom where he heard the shower running. He figured Joanna was in there, getting ready for bed.

The house was silent, and he stood outside the door for a long couple of minutes. His dad always had a way, just like his granddad had, of cutting to the core of the matter. Walking down to his room, he passed it by and went to hers, slipping inside to wait for her.

9

JOANNA HATED CRYING. SHE'D cried buckets when her mom had left, but she'd been seven. Even then, she had tried not to let anyone see.

She'd also vowed after that that she'd cried enough for a long, long time.

She hadn't even given in to tears when she'd been shot, and she had only shed a few embarrassing tears at her brother's wedding, which she hoped no one had noticed. But it took every ounce of control she had just to make it to the shower where she could let go for a few minutes. It had just been too much. Ben's passionate words at the pond, the way he moved her. His family, his parents being so nice to her, welcoming her into their home, their faces lit with hope for their son, because of her.

And she was lying to all of them. Well, mostly. She hadn't lied when she admitted to Ben that what she felt for him was more than sex, too. She probably shouldn't have opened that door, but the words had come out before she could stop them.

Anger blended into the mix of emotions running

through her as she thought about why she'd been given this assignment, not to mention Don's warning about her career.

She'd been devoted to her work to the point of almost dying, and still she had to prove herself. What did she have to show for it? None of this, she thought miserably, looking at the beautiful tile along the edges of the bathroom that Ben's mother had proudly showed her. She and Hank had built their life here, updated the entire place themselves.

A testament to family and to love. A legacy. Jarod was building that now with Lacey, and even her dad had someone in his life.

All Joanna had was lies.

She'd put some terrible criminals behind bars. Kept society safe, but what did she have when she went home at night?

It had never bothered her before, but now, faced with her emotions and the prospect—the very real prospect—that she was going to lose Ben, all the walls she built around herself felt brittle.

She straightened, taking hold of her crazy emotions. It was her job, and right now, she was all that stood between these good people and something bad.

Letting herself forget why she was here, even for a few hours, even for a day, was foolish. She'd had fun. She'd let herself stare into his eyes, kiss his fingers. She let down her guard, and she'd been burned.

Joanna liked his parents. Rachel was the kind of mother Joanna had fantasized about after her own had left, and Hank was a good man. She could see Ben was like both of them. Steady, solid, good.

There wasn't a way for her to fit into their world.

In the kitchen, the four of them downstairs, it had been far too easy to imagine how wonderful a real life like the one Ben enjoyed could be—one full of sunshine, picnics and family.

It had scared the crap out of her when she'd seen that knowing look in his parents' eyes. The warm acceptance, the way they'd included her and seemed to like her.

Stepping out of the shower, she pulled on the light robe that Rachel had given her and padded down to the room to get dressed, only to find herself face to face with Ben when she opened the door.

He was in bed. His jeans were on the floor. Her mind blanked.

"Hey, gorgeous," he said, smiling at her in a way that made her knees weak.

Then he looked closer. "Are you okay? Were you crying?" he asked, getting out of bed to close the distance between them, tipping her face up, his eyes fierce.

"I wasn't. Just got shampoo in my eyes," she said, but even as she did, hot tears prickled at the back of her eyelids, and she silently cursed, trying to fight them back.

"Yeah, I don't think so, c'mon," he said, putting an arm around her shoulder. "What's going on? I could tell down in the kitchen you were about ready to run out the door. You can tell me."

Every word he spoke was a stab in the gut. He was being so good to her.

"Ben, we have to talk. This isn't working, I can't—"

"Listen, I don't know what happened, but I want to know. Sure, this has all happened fast, and it's scary. For me, too. No one else has made me feel like you do."

She took a deep breath. "It did freak me out," she confessed. "Being here, your parents, who are great, by the way, but—"

"I know. They like you, and they are blinded by the visions of grandchildren dancing before them," he said with a smile, shaking his head ruefully. "Don't worry. I told Dad straight that we were new to each other, not to push. Don't let it get to you."

She let out the breath she was holding, relaxing a bit, feeling silly. "I know, I'm sorry. They really are wonderful, but suddenly it was all just so—"

"Much."

"Yeah."

"Well, if you feel that with me, let me know," he whispered in her ear, dragging his tongue along the edge of the shell, making her eyes close and her head fall back toward him. "I'll back off, I promise."

She had started to tell him that was the last thing she wanted when they both spun around, hearing shouting, downstairs.

"That's Dad," Ben said, lurching away, grabbing his jeans and yanking them on, heading out the door. Joanna got her gun from her bag and ran out behind him.

"What's going on?" he asked as he ran down the stairs, seeing his mom wrapped in her robe over her pajamas, heading out the front door.

"There's a fire in the back barn," she said, looking worried and taking off after his father.

He turned, surprised to see Joanna dash past him, shouting at the two of them to stay in the house in a way that made them all freeze in their tracks. He followed, grabbing her by her arm and spinning her to face him.

She easily disengaged and pushed him back, her eyes intense.

"Joanna, what the hell?" he asked, looking down toward the burning building where his father had gone, the sound of sirens still far off in the distance.

"Get back in the house, Ben, and keep your mom there, too, and I'll go after your dad," she said, and only then did he notice the .45 in her hand. She shoved her badge up to his face where he could see it, her expression stony.

"I'm a U.S. Marshal, Ben. I'm here to protect you. I can explain more later. I don't know what this is—it could be a trap, so please, get back in the house, lock up somewhere, and let me go do my job."

In a second, before he could form his next thought, she was gone.

JOANNA STUDIED THE SCENE, HER eyes traveling over the mostly intact barn—the fire hadn't gone too far, amazingly, and had only consumed part of one corner of the massive old structure before the volunteers had put it out.

That alone pointed to arson. There was nothing else that could have started the fire—no lightning, no electricity in the barn, no accelerants left lying around—no reason a fire should have started in that quadrant, although the odor of chemicals, not gas, was clear in the afterburn. Chemical analysis would tell them what they were later. Luckily, the barn was used only for equipment storage, not animals.

The fire officer who stood surveying the scene with her had reached the same preliminary conclusion—arson—not entirely because of the forensics. Some other vandalism had made it clear that there'd been an intruder on the ranch.

"The weird thing is, why would the arsonist slash all the tires of the cars in the driveway, but set fire to a barn that was the farthest away from the house? Why not set fire to the house? And what did slashing the tires accomplish?"

The guy seemed genuinely confused, and Joanna nodded.

"Maybe a former employee, or someone who was angry about something that happened at the party yesterday—maybe they weren't invited," she joked, though that wasn't what she thought at all.

What she believed was that the slashed tires and the fire were a message. A warning, the way she saw it. She knew from the look on Ben's face when he saw the tires that he thought the same thing.

Still, the fire officer had a point, and she wasn't completely settled on what had happened here. Some things were just…off.

She couldn't figure it out now, and while a few of the firemen would stay on site until they were sure nothing would reignite, there was nothing else she could do for the moment.

Rachel had been cooking all night, feeding firefighters and sending breakfast down for the people at the barn. It was how she dealt with stress, apparently.

Joanna was starving, something she hadn't realized until Lisa came walking toward the barn with another thermos of coffee, handing it to one of the guys before coming over to join Joanna.

"Coming up for breakfast? Rachel has enough food up there to feed an army."

Joanna was surprised any of them were speaking to her.

"I don't think I should," she said, not looking Lisa in the eye. "But thanks."

Lisa shuddered. "I can't imagine why anyone would want to do such a thing to the Callahans. They've never hurt anyone in their lives."

"Yeah. Who knows what prompts people to do these things."

"I know what prompts Ben," Lisa said with a grin. "He's been driving us crazy pacing back and forth to the window keeping his eye on you down here with the firemen," she said.

"Lisa, do you know what happened last night? I mean, with me?"

"Yeah, Ben told everyone what's going on and who you are. He's totally pissed. But the way I see it, you are just doing your job, and if he knew who you were, he never would have gone along with it," Lisa said with a shrug. "Men."

Joanna smiled, and shook her head. "I was pretty sure everyone would hate my guts for lying."

"Nah, and neither does Ben, but you know, I guess I can see how it makes things more complicated with you two."

Joanna started to argue, but then considered the cat was out of the bag in a lot of ways. "Yeah, I guess it does. Or not. There is no 'us two' anymore, I don't think."

"Well, just hang in there. You can handle him," Lisa said confidently, and smiled up at Joanna. "You *are* a U.S. Marshal after all."

Joanna blew out a breath. "That I am."

"You should know, though, Charlie says maybe Ben should think about not testifying. And I think Ben is considering it."

Joanna stopped in her tracks. "Really? Why would anyone think that? Ben has to put these guys away, if he can. They killed someone."

"But they're strangers, not family. I have to admit, as much as I know Ben wants to do the right thing, if it means risking his family's safety, how can he? The law will just have to do its job."

Joanna stifled another groan. She couldn't let them talk Ben out of testifying—not over this. Which made her mind leap to another place as they walked the rest of the distance to the house. Her appetite had diminished considerably under the weight of her thoughts as they entered the kitchen, though the aromas of the food were tantalizing.

Rachel met her with a steaming-hot cup of coffee and pointed her to several warming pans full of waffles, bacon, sausage and home fries, among other things. She still treated Joanna warmly, though Joanna could tell by the worried look in her eyes that things had changed.

No grandbabies were popping up in Rachel's imagination now, Joanna figured.

She offered a brief hello to Hank and Charlie, who nodded in response, and then she met Ben's eyes across the kitchen. Everything they'd shared flashed through her mind, along with an aching need to go to him, to make things right, but that was probably not going to happen.

She went to the counter where he was, and filled a

plate with some of the food, although she was barely paying attention.

"You doing okay?"

"Fine," he said.

"Right."

"What did you find?" he asked.

"Nothing much new. They have to do some tests, but it's pretty clear someone set the fire, probably to discourage you from testifying," she said. "So are you discouraged?"

"I don't know yet," he replied.

"That's good. Let me know what I can do to encourage you not to change your mind."

"I think you've done enough, thanks," he said coolly and left her gaping.

After a shocked second, during which the kitchen had gone completely silent, she slammed her plate down on the counter and went after him, finding him in the front room, staring out a window.

"I get it, this stinks, but you can't walk away from your testimony because you're pissed at me," she said. "Even if you did refuse to testify, you'll never be truly safe, and neither will they," she said, nodding back toward the kitchen, where she was sure they could hear every word. "You're a loose end. You know as well as I do that guys like this don't like loose ends."

His back was ramrod-straight, his hands jammed in his pockets. When he turned to face her, she could tell he was exhausted—none of them had slept all night.

Correction—she and Ben hadn't slept for the last two nights, she remembered with embarrassing clarity.

"Two guys came after me," he said baldly.

"What? When?"

"Thursday night. When I went out for a run."

She thought back, remembering the scrapes and bruises. "You said…"

"Yeah, well, I can lie, too," he responded. "The blood on the shirt was from one of them…" he paused, realization dawning. "I see. That was why you took it. To test it." He barked out a laugh, shaking his head, muttering something to himself about being a damned fool.

It took everything she had to steer away from the personal and to keep the discussion on track.

"So with the two guys. What happened?"

He filled her in succinctly, and it took everything she had to listen without reacting. He could have been killed.

"I put both of them down—figuratively speaking—but their IDs were fake, the car a rental. No leads there," he said.

"How can you know? You should have reported that to the marshals, immediately," she said, her voice rising.

"So you could put me into federal custody? I don't think so. Besides, what if they weren't even connected to your case?"

"You have more than one group of bad guys after you?" she asked incredulously.

His expression became veiled in a way she'd never quite seen before. "It's possible. I have a lot of nasty people in my past."

She was quiet while digesting that. "Okay, well, even if that was the case, what then?"

"There is no 'what then.' I took care of it, and now they know I'm on to them, that I'd be aware."

"You think that's better?" She gaped at him in shock.

"Yeah. It is. Harder for them to sneak up on you when you know they're coming."

"You've got to be kidding. Do you have any idea how bad this could be for you?" Joanna said, staring at him incredulously. "Interfering in a federal investigation. Withholding and tampering with evidence." She stared at him. "I should just cuff you now and haul your ass into custody."

The look he sent her suggested she try it.

"You need to trust the law to do the job, Ben. Let me do my job."

"The law didn't do its job last night!" he accused, stepping forward.

She processed everything he was saying, irrationally turned on by the friction between them, the way his nostrils flared, the tense hold of a hard male body she knew intimately. But he was wrong.

"It's a lot more difficult with an uncooperative witness. If you had consented to protection in the first place, or let us know about the men following you, we could have been watching more closely, and maybe it wouldn't have happened at all."

"All your office offered me was living at a safehouse for a month, which left everyone here vulnerable. You know the first thing I would do if I were these guys? If I wanted to gain leverage? I'd come after my family, friends, no matter where I was hiding. There was no way my parents could leave the ranch, or Charlie and Lisa leave their jobs, the kids, to get out of harm's way."

"I get that, but why not allow one of us to be here?"

"One person can't watch all of us twenty-four seven, and you've proven that. And you were watching me about as closely as you possibly could," he added silkily.

The barb hit its mark, but she sucked it up for the time being.

"Don't make this about you and me. Right now—"

"Don't make it about you and me? Are you kidding? We've been about as 'you and me' as two people can be, or was having sex with me part of your job? Were you sleeping with me only to keep a closer eye on me, because if I'd known that was part of witness protection in the first place, maybe I would have changed my mind—"

Joanna took a deep breath, tipping her chin up, and taking a few steps closer. She would not be intimidated by him. She was pretty sure her status was shredded and that he had no respect for her personally or for her authority, but she maintained her position anyway, giving him his options with a level stare.

"Think about this carefully, Ben. That killer could walk. You're the only witness. I hope you aren't serious about reconsidering your testimony."

"I'm not stupid, Joanna," he said stiffly. "I know they will use my testimony to pressure him into giving up his bosses for a plea deal—so he walks with or without me. Probably shuttled off somewhere safely to a new life through WITSEC."

She couldn't argue. That was probably exactly what would happen. "But the bigger organization behind him will be taken down."

Ben shook his head. "I just don't know. I don't know who to trust anymore."

She took a breath, hurt seeping through her, too

aware of the silence around her as Ben's family looked on.

"Fine. Let me know by day's end what you want to do. But remember, if you refuse to testify, they're still out there, and the government will no longer offer any protection. For any of you," she added, making eye contact with the others.

No one said a word. Good. She didn't want to hear anything. Her phone rang, and she checked to see Don's name.

Without another word, she walked out the front door.

"Yeah, Don."

"Things under control out there?"

She closed her eyes. "Not so much."

"Need help?"

"Ben…Callahan, he's pretty angry, and he's up in the air about his testimony. I told him not to make a rash decision, and I'm working on getting him to make the right one."

Don cursed under his breath. "I think it's better for you to come in, and I'll send someone else out—you're probably not exactly on this guy's Christmas list right now."

"I don't think—"

"I wasn't asking your permission, Jo."

Joanna couldn't leave Ben. She had to convince him to testify, to be here in case something happened… maybe to try to make things right.

"I have vacation time."

"What?"

"I'm asking for my vacation time. You guys have been pushing me into taking more time off until the whole other mess was settled, so I am. As of right now."

"Jo, you can't be serious," Don said in a warning tone.

"Consider this my official request for time off. I have it coming to me, and you know it. And if you don't give it to me, then…I quit."

"Joanna, you're not thinking straight here, why on earth would you want to—" He shut up suddenly as he realized why, and Joanna swallowed hard. "So that's how it is. Damn, Jo, could this get any worse?"

"Oh, probably," she said with a half-hearted laugh.

"Forget it. I can't have you running around there off-duty, half-cocked. At least if you're still on assignment, I can keep my eye on you."

"So you'll let me deal with this?"

"I'm going against every bit of common sense I have, but yes. If anything happens, you will be standing in some majorly deep cow manure."

"Loud and clear."

"I hope he's worth it, Jo."

"I guess we'll see."

Walking blindly away, she needed to get some distance from Ben, Don and everyone else, just for a short time.

She found herself, annoyingly, at the pond where she and Ben had been the night before.

Great choice, she thought, kicking herself mentally as she sat down on a rock, getting her wits about her as she dialed another number and waited for her brother to answer the line.

"Hey, jelly bean, what's up? Done with your assignment?" Jarod asked, sounding chipper.

The tears she'd managed to hold at bay—for years, maybe—decided all to come forth with the force of a category-five hurricane. She could barely get a word out to her brother until the storm passed.

"Jarod, I really messed up," she said miserably, and told him everything.

BEN WAS BEAT AND HAD BEEN standing there staring at himself in the bathroom mirror, unshaven, for about ten minutes. His mind had been in high gear all night, thinking about everything, especially about Joanna in bed in the apartment, alone...probably wearing next to nothing. All he had to do was take a deep breath and he could imagine her scent, how soft she was.

He was dying to touch her, but kept reminding himself that he'd never really known her in the first place. The Joanna he'd thought he knew was a lie. How could he have been so stupid? He'd seen some of the signs, but he had ignored them. It was clear she'd do whatever it took to get her job done, even if that meant screwing him in whatever way she had to.

So was that all it was? Her sex play was just distraction? A ploy?

Even as he thought it, it didn't feel right to think of her that way.

So what? She had a job to do. She did it. Just like you did a hundred times, his inner voice chided him.

But he'd never slept with any of his mission targets.

He'd been having the same argument with himself over and over again, wavering between longing, anger and frustration for the past twenty-four hours until he was sick and tired of it.

Slamming the door, he went downstairs to go to the bar, and stopped short, finding Joanna sitting on his sofa, staring him in the eye.

"Why are you here?"

"Where are you going?"

The both asked at the same time. She stood, looking beautiful, but totally exhausted.

"Were you here all night?"

"That's my job," she said lightly. "I haven't done a great job of it lately, but I'm hoping to improve. You heading over to the bar?"

"Yeah."

"I'll go first, check it out. You follow."

He didn't argue, though he felt ridiculous waiting in the doorway, wondering if this meant Joanna was going soon.

"I thought you'd have left," he said lamely, and then realized how relieved he was that she hadn't. The thought unsettled him more than he expected, not being able to see her again. Gone, as though she had never been there at all.

"As long as you're still a witness, I plan to do my job. My focus is on you, Charlie and Lisa. My supervisor is sending a second marshal, Cal Stivers, to stay with your parents. I think we owe you that."

"What if I don't want you here?" he asked, and thought he might have seen a flinch in her expression, but so quickly that he might have just imagined it.

"Then they can send someone else, no problem. But I'd like to see this through, if you don't mind. I want to finish the job."

"And if I decide not to testify?"

"Then we go home, and this is over. But I would advise you to testify. You know it's the right thing to do, and you know as well as I do that it's the only sure way to get these guys out of your hair."

"I still have to think on it," he said.

"I'll stay with you until we get you to court. The trial is at the end of next week—I think we can both do what we have to do for that long. But if you decide to step down, we need to know sooner rather than later so that the attorneys can do what they have to do."

"Sure, I'll let you know," he said as she nodded and turned her back, walking away as they came out into the bar. It was surreal. Yesterday, he'd been as close to her as a man and woman could be, physically, anyway. Today, she was so distant, it seemed as if he didn't know her at all.

Maybe he didn't.

"I GUESS LISA WAS RIGHT," Charlie said from behind the bar, and Ben turned to find his friend staring at him.

"How's that?"

"You're crazy about her."

"She makes me crazy, that much is true," Ben murmured.

"Find out anything else about the fire?" Charlie asked.

"Nope. Nothing that will lead us to who did it. Who knows, could have just been kids starting trouble, someone passing through, guess there's no way to know."

"Or the guys who you're testifying against. Sure seems like a message to me."

"Yeah, or that."

"You still gonna do it? Testify?"

Ben started to say yes, and then paused. "I'm not sure."

Charlie looked at him, curiously hopeful. Ben studied his friend. Charlie always had a rotten poker face.

"What's up, Charlie?"

"Sorry, Ben. Just that, well, you know Lisa and I have been seeing each other."

"And I'm glad for you, so don't break up with her—if it's between her going or you, it's going to be you," Ben teased.

"No worry on either score. Her divorce goes through, we're getting hitched."

Ben pulled back in surprise. "Are you kidding? When did this happen?"

"It hasn't yet, but I'm going to ask her."

Ben could see in his friend's face that he was lighting up from the inside out, but there was still something bugging him. Even Ben could feel his friend's worry.

"Well, I couldn't be happier for you, and Lisa deserves a nice guy, and so do those kids. So what's wrong?"

"Just…this thing with you and testifying. Like you said, we're all in danger now, until it's over. I don't care about me, but Lisa, you know, and the kids… I can't take even the slightest chance that they could get hurt."

"Understandable."

Charlie looked away, setting his hands on the bar. "I know it's selfish, and I know you need to do the right thing, but I wish you wouldn't testify, and I hate saying that. But I just can't help thinking that if something happened to her…well, how would you feel if something happened to Joanna?"

Ben was thrown off by his friend's question. In spite of being ticked-off at Joanna, the same protective feelings came rushing to the fore when he thought about her being hurt.

He didn't want to feel that way for her, but he couldn't seem to help it.

"Would it be worth it? Testifying? I mean, after all, you said they might let the guy free, the killer you saw, so what's the point?" Charlie continued to press, and Ben admitted that he'd had that same thought. What was the point of being a political pawn for the Justice Department, and risking putting everyone he loved in danger?

Ben's inner sense of right and wrong dictated he do something, not just stand idly by, but he also hated having the people he cared about worried and in possible danger. That was a good reason to get this over with and put it behind them once and for all.

Joanna was still here, and that couldn't be easy for her. And they had sent someone to watch the ranch… it made him feel better to know that. He'd been foolish to think he could handle it all himself, and though Ben understood Charlie's concern, he didn't know if he could turn his back on the case. He was also relieved Joanna was still here, for many reasons, and refusing to testify meant he'd lose her, permanently. That probably shouldn't figure into his decision, but it did.

"If you think I should give Lisa some time off until this is done, I can do that—"

Charlie put his hand up. "No. She needs the money, even with both our checks," he objected. "Just…think about it."

Ben nodded, though he more or less had made up his mind to go ahead with testifying—not that he was going to say so directly to anyone, even Joanna, yet.

"I think about little else these days."

Ben knew why Charlie thought the way he did. The guy had the worst childhood ever, and the only family he'd known was Ben's and the army. Now, he had the chance to have a real family, and Ben couldn't blame him for wanting to protect them.

He watched in amazement as Joanna grabbed a tray of condiments and started setting tables for lunch, smiling as she received an enthusiastic hug from Lisa, who seemed just as happy to see her there.

Joanna's smile in response seemed genuine. Maybe it hadn't all been a lie?

Ben was getting a hell of a headache when the kitchen door behind him opened, and he looked up to see his dad.

"Hey, Dad, this is a surprise," he said, turning to greet his father.

"Thought I'd come by and see how you were doing, and Joanna, as well," Hank said, his eyes catching where she still stood with Lisa.

"I'm glad you came by. Want some lunch?"

"I wouldn't say no," his father responded, and Ben clasped his shoulder, laughing as they walked back to the kitchen. His father never turned down barbecue.

"Had to practically arm wrestle the marshal they sent, a guy named Stivers, to get him to let me drive down here," his father said as Ben dished out a few plates and brought them to the lounge where his father was already seated.

Ben took the chair opposite him and said, "They do take their job seriously."

"They didn't make marshals who looked like her

when I was growing up. If they had, I might have gotten in more trouble," his father joked.

"Don't let Mom hear you say that," Ben said, smiling, and pushed a plate over to him.

"Gotta be tough for a woman in that line of work. Just as capable, but have to prove themselves all the time," Hank said, taking a large bite of his sandwich.

"Dad, let's not go there. I know she had a job to do, but she lied to me when we were…getting involved."

"Yeah, I know that was a blow, but it doesn't mean she wasn't in a tough position herself."

"She could have said no."

"So could you."

"I didn't know she wasn't who she said she was!" Ben exclaimed, putting his sandwich down. "I just thought she was a waitress. A smart, funny, sexy woman who I was starting to—"

"Yeah, I know, son. So does her being a marshal change any of that for you? Really?"

"I feel like I don't know her."

"You could change that pretty easily. I guess you have to decide what you're going to do about her."

"How so?"

"Well, that's for you to figure out. But I was curious myself, and went poking around the internet. I printed you a copy," his father said, pushing some papers across the table to Ben.

"An outstanding woman, I think you'll agree," Hank said, watching Ben closely as he looked at the papers.

Ben looked through them, a collection of old articles about Joanna that had been in the news, on the internet, including several commendations by the Justice

Department, and one story about her being shot in the line of duty a few months ago.

There weren't too many details, but Ben stared at the picture of her being loaded into the ambulance that the photographers had managed to snap; the caption read, U.S. Marshal Shot by Serial Rapist.

Ben's stomach plummeted.

"She puts her life on the line, Ben, the same way you did all those years. She was putting her life on the line for you," his father said emphatically. "I'd think you could cut her a little slack."

Ben didn't say anything, but kept reading, his mind scrambling. Joanna had nearly died going after a serial rapist who had killed two women, and had almost killed her, the article said.

"I never thought you'd find a woman equal to you, Ben, but it looks like you have," Hank said, sitting down to finish his sandwich. "Be a shame if you just let her walk away."

"I don't know, Dad. It could be too late for any of that."

"It's never too late to work it out, if you want to try." Hank sighed, patting his stomach. "Thanks for the lunch. I have to get back to the ranch. We're down two hands, and things are kind of nuts around there right now and Marshal Stivers will probably send in the troops if I'm not back when I said I would be."

"I'm glad he's there. It's a weight off my mind, I'll admit. Thanks, Dad," Ben said, though he wasn't quite sure what his father expected him to do about Joanna. His dad left him deep in thought.

He knew he wanted her, but everything had changed between them. Or had it?

He supposed there was only one way to find out.

CHARLIE WATCHED THROUGH THE open doorway as Abe focused on his homework at the dining-room table, his smooth brow wrinkled in concentration, his grip on the pencil extremely tight as he wrote the names of states and capitals into the blank map given to him by his teacher.

Charlie had offered to help—the kid had so much homework for his age that it seemed criminal—but Abe was intent on doing his own work. He liked school, said he wanted to be a veterinarian when he was older, and so he had to do well in his classes.

Patsy's voice burbled like bubbles in a stream from the floor beside her brother, where she was playing with her dolls, making them talk to each other.

Charlie loved them both about as much as he was able, which was a lot.

"He's so focused for his age," he said to Lisa, grabbing a towel to help dry the dishes as they stood a few yards away in the kitchen after dinner.

He tried to help around the house as much as possible, especially because the first time he had picked up a dish towel, Lisa had been so amazed and grateful that she'd made him a pie. It was crazy, but she'd never had a man help her in the house. Her ex seemed to go out of his way to make life more miserable rather than easier, and Charlie wanted to show her that men could be different.

She made him want to be different. Better.

"Did you like school at his age?" she asked, scrubbing out a pot.

"No way. Wanted to be out playing, doing anything but sitting still."

He'd certainly never had anyone to help him with homework, or make him a nice dinner, not after his mom died when he was almost too young to remember her.

"Playing soldier, no doubt."

"Absolutely. Ben and I would build forts from old wood in the desert on his family's land, and sometimes we'd even camp out there, preparing for night-time invasions," he said, laughing.

"Ever get invaded?"

"Only by the local wildlife," he said, grinning.

"It's so nice you two have been close all your lives… parted ways, and now you're back together again," she said happily.

"Yeah, he's more like a brother," Charlie admitted as Lisa went out to the dining room to move the kids along, getting ready for bed.

He loved being a part of it all. Loved sitting down to dinner, helping with bedtime, reading stories to the kids or doing stuff around the place. It was the family he'd always imagined having, being a part of, and he knew they loved him too, which was the most amazing part.

When he was a kid, most of his meals were skipped or stolen, which was how he got to be friends with Ben, actually. He'd been nailed for the nth time stealing lunch at school, when Ben had told the lunch lady that Charlie wasn't stealing it, Ben was paying for it. Charlie wasn't too proud to accept the helping hand.

After a while, Charlie spent more time with Ben's family than at home. Rachel had made him dinners and desserts and let him sleep in the clean room upstairs so often he should have paid rent, but the Callahans always welcomed him.

Charlie signed up for the military as soon as Ben did. He hadn't really wanted to go that way, but college wasn't for him, and as it ended up, the army was good for him. Turned him into a man.

He and Ben had lost touch a lot over those years, but now it was as if the time had never passed. Charlie swallowed the stab of guilt he had been fighting ever since he'd sneaked back after the party, set that fire, slashed the tires two nights ago.

What other choice did he have? He made sure it wasn't going to be serious, no one would be hurt, no real damage done, but maybe Ben would take it as a warning—which he had—and back off of his testimony. Then they would all be okay. Of course, now there was Joanna to consider. Did she suspect anything? Charlie thought she had sent him a few strange looks that afternoon at work, and wondered if she knew more than she was telling anyone. She'd fooled everyone, and fooling Ben wasn't easy. What if she knew?

No. If she knew, he wouldn't be standing here right now.

He fought the surge of betrayal by telling himself that it was to protect Ben as much as anyone. If they sent anyone else...Charlie could convince him not to testify, to save Ben's life. Charlie had to make it all stop, and if anything was going to work, it was making Ben believe the people he loved were in danger. Ben would do anything to avoid that.

"I was glad to see Joanna stayed," Lisa said, resting against the counter, drying her hands.

"Really?" Charlie asked. He had been less than thrilled. He liked her well enough when he thought she was a waitress, but now she was a threat. Ben still looked at her as if she was the center of the universe, and that could mess things up considerably.

"I know Ben had the hots for her, and I wondered if

he'd scratched that itch—" he said, but his mind was buzzing again with ways he might be able to discourage Ben from testifying.

"Geez, Charlie," she said, laughing and snapping the end of a towel at him. It hit his artificial leg, so he didn't feel a thing and stuck his tongue out at her.

"Stick that out only if you mean to use it," she said with a sassy wink.

"If you say so," he said with a playful leer and grabbed her, hauling her up close for a deep, strawberry-flavored kiss from the shortcake she'd made for dessert.

She kissed him once again, and backed away. "But seriously, I think they have something more than the hots for each other. Do you see how they look at each other?"

Charlie scoffed. "Guys don't notice that kind of thing."

"Well, take it from me, I think they might have something serious going on."

"Seems a little quick," Charlie said.

"Doesn't take long when you meet the right one." Lisa returned to his arms after she put the last dish away.

Charlie heard the bath water running upstairs, and knew they'd have to go up in a minute to watch over bath time, and get everyone settled in. He gave Lisa a quick taste of what he hoped to do with her after the kids were in bed.

She pressed into him, making him hard and humble at the same time. He didn't know he could love someone this much, or be loved back.

The black fear in the pit of his stomach was because of how fast that would change if she found out about his past addiction and what he was up to now. He had to make sure that never happened. He didn't deserve to lose everything, not again.

If only Ben hadn't seen that stupid murder, everything would be perfect.

The fire had almost done the trick though. Maybe one more nudge would get him to go the rest of the way, then they would all be free to be happy.

"So you think Ben is really falling for Joanna?" Charlie asked Lisa, pulling her in close to him for a tight hug.

"I do. And she's falling for him, too, though she wouldn't quite admit it, but it was all over her face."

"Well, that's good," Charlie said quietly, an idea forming. That could be just what he needed to make Ben turn over. He'd seen Ben's face when he'd mentioned something happening to Joanna. Maybe she was just the one to make him change his mind.

"Wouldn't it be great? The four of us together? What if they decided to get married? Then we could all have a ceremony togeth—" Lisa stopped looking horrified.

"What? What's the matter?"

"Oh, Charlie, I'm sorry, I'm not even really divorced yet, and here I had you walking down the aisle with me," she said hastily.

Charlie laughed, noting the mortified expression on her pretty face.

"Did you just propose to me, then?"

"I know, I didn't mean it, I was just thinking how nice it would be, with Ben and Joanna, and if things worked out like that," she babbled, and dropped her head into her hands. "I wouldn't blame you if you were running out the door about now," she said.

"I'm not running anywhere, darlin'. I love you, and

I love those two mini-yous upstairs, and there is no place I'd rather be than here. And when your divorce comes through, you pick the time and the place, and I'm there," he said, his heart full.

Lisa looked surprised all over again.

"Charlie, did you just accept my proposal?" she said breathlessly.

"I absolutely did," he said, and was nearly deafened by the whoop of joy she let out, followed by the stampede of footsteps down the stairs as the kids ran into the kitchen.

"What? What's going on?" Abe asked, searching their faces for any clue.

"Charlie just made me the happiest woman on the planet," Lisa told the kids.

"Did he give you chocolate?" Patsy asked, and they all laughed.

"A motorcycle?" Abe guessed.

"Even better, but we'll talk about it more later," Lisa said, all smiles and ruffling the boy's hair, hugging them both tightly. "Right now, time for bed."

She looked over the children's heads toward Charlie, her eyes beckoning, and Charlie joined them, wrapping his arms around all three, and knowing he would do whatever it took to defend this family. *His* family.

He'd keep them safe, no matter what.

10

JOANNA WENT THROUGH HER YOGA routine in the middle of Ben's living-room floor, wringing the tension from her muscles by stretching them to the limit.

It had been a long afternoon, and she needed a break. Ben too, apparently. He'd gone upstairs for a shower and hadn't come back down. But she heard him rustling around. Joanna knew he was annoyed with her being there, however, now she was doing her job the way it was supposed to be done. No more pretense. She was going to be on him like peanut butter on jelly. So to speak.

Laying back in *Savasana,* the restful pose that always ended a yoga session, she closed her eyes and groaned, all of the tension returning.

Ben hadn't said a word to her when she'd arrived. She'd checked in briefly with Stivers, who was watching the ranch, and everything else was calm, now. As if there had never been any trouble at all.

In her experience, that's when things tended to explode in your face.

Joanna took a deep breath, then another, trying to

direct the in-breath to certain parts of her body, and then exhaling in a calm way, letting her limbs grow heavy.

Yoga wasn't something she'd discovered on her own, or even had done voluntarily. Department of Defense and some arms of the military were using it for conditioning as well as treatment for post-traumatic stress syndrome—with good success—and so some law-enforcement departments were picking it up as well.

Hers had been mandatory treatment assigned by her physical therapist to help her shoulder regain its strength and flexibility. While Joanna had resisted at first, thinking it had to be a bunch of New Age nonsense and fluff, she found out differently very quickly. Her yoga workouts were among the hardest she'd ever had, testing muscles she never knew were there, and she had carried on classes and personal practice long past her recuperation. She smiled to herself, recalling her attempts to get her brother to try it. That had been amusing, but not very successful.

Under the right conditions, it did help her relax and focus—and that helped her become better at her job.

But it wasn't going to help today.

Giving in, she pushed up from the floor, intending to shower, as well. She saw a light on under the door to Ben's room, and she knocked softly.

He answered, clad only in shorts, his skin and hair still damp. Desire hit her like a fist, and she had to take a breath before speaking.

"I'll be in the shower. Don't leave the house," she said, sounding more terse than she meant to.

He looked down at himself, and waved the book in his hand. "I'm in for the night."

"Okay. I'll be out in fifteen minutes, and back downstairs."

"Why don't you take the room down the hall, Jo, it—"

She shook her head. "I'd rather keep an eye on the first floor, and it makes it easier to go outside, check there too. The divan is comfortable if I need a snooze," she said, realizing her error a second too late as her eyes met his and she knew they were both thinking about what had happened on that divan just days ago.

"I'll be downstairs if you need me," she said and turned away.

"Oh, I need you. I just don't know what to do about it."

At first, she wasn't sure she'd actually heard that, and paused in the hall, letting the words and the sexy tone of his voice sink in.

She faced him squarely. "You don't need to worry about that. We won't be doing anything about it. This is work only, no funny business, remember?"

"But you could keep a much closer eye on me in here," he said seductively, and she narrowed her eyes.

"Are you messing with me or what?"

He stared at her for a long minute, and it threw her that she was trembling. The idea that he still wanted her, wanted anything to do with her, turned the world upside down.

Maybe that's what he was trying to do? Was this some new game? Some kind of payback? Answer his bedroom door half-dressed and tease, then back off?

"You know me better than that, Joanna. I don't play games," he said, looking deeply at her, and opening the door a little more widely.

Was it an invitation, or a dare?

His eyes reminded her of so many things she loved. The desert sands, caramel, whiskey, lions, butter rum ice cream and topaz. Depending on the light and his mood, they changed intensity, and right now they didn't flash in anger or agitation, but were quiet, contemplative and definitely hot.

He leaned on the doorjamb, looking at her lazily.

"Why are you acting like this?" she said impatiently.

"I had a talk with my dad today, and it cleared my head, I guess. I didn't like that you lied to me, but I know you were only doing your job, and I know it's a serious job. You had to follow orders. I get that, and I don't see why it should come between us now."

Her heart leapt, but she kept her mind steady.

"I can. I have a job to do, and I can't do it if I'm…if we're…you know."

He smiled a little. "If we're what, Jo?"

"Sleeping together," she said, straightening stiffly.

"We slept a little, but the stuff we did when we were awake was a lot more fun," he said, looking dangerous.

"I'm taking my shower," she said, needing to end this conversation. He was playing with her, and she was either going to hit him or jump him any second now, and neither was a good idea.

"If you change your mind…"

It was all she heard before she closed the door behind her more loudly than she intended. She took a breath, her jaw clenched. She didn't like letting him know he'd gotten to her at all, but who was she kidding?

Stepping into the shower, she turned the water on cold and didn't warm it up until her head was clear and her teeth were chattering. Washing her hair and soaping up, she wondered, for the first time, if she could do this.

It was easier if he was angry at her, not speaking to her, keeping his distance. But if he changed his plan of attack—and that was what it had felt like—she'd have a much harder time resisting.

Because she cared more than she wanted to. Wanted him more than she cared to.

If she were smart, she'd take herself off the case, tell Don to send in someone else, the way he had wanted to in the first place. But with her next thought, she knew she couldn't do it. Couldn't admit that she couldn't handle it; she had to see it through.

She was so caught up in her own thoughts she didn't hear the door open and shut, and was startled when he pulled the curtain back, standing there before her as naked as she was.

"Ben!"

She was sputtering as he stepped inside the tub and took her in his arms. His kiss wiped out any thought that might have followed her exclamation. Her hands were planted on his chest, and she knew she should push him away, but instead, her fingers curled as his tongue rubbed up against hers, getting reacquainted.

Other parts wanted to get familiar, as well, his thigh nudging in between hers, his hands covering her breasts.

"Ben, we can't—" she managed as he broke the kiss, only to take his lips to her breast, lowering his hand to cause trouble between her legs.

He stroked her hard, sucking hard, bringing her to the edge of a sharp climax that had her shaking and clutching his shoulders for balance. Then he stopped, stood, and her knees almost gave out.

"If you don't want this, Joanna, then go. But if you stay, I'm not stopping," he said, his own breath heavy, his voice rough.

Leaving would have taken more strength than she had, she realized sadly. She wanted him, one more time, just one more time when they both knew the truth, and everything was out in the open. Then they'd be done.

"Don't stop," she whispered, and took his hand, putting it back against her tender skin as she sought his mouth.

She came seconds later, crying her pleasure into his mouth as he kissed her, and reveled in his control, the masterfulness of his touch as he brought her back up again.

"I couldn't spend one more night thinking about this with you downstairs, and me alone, hard, aching, up here," he said, turning her to face the shower wall. She planted her hands, lifting her hips, knowing what he wanted.

"I ached, too," she admitted, sighing as he eased into her, filling her until she felt she'd burst wide open.

She thought, perhaps, given her deception, the situation, that he needed to be in control, and she was fine with that. Holding her hips with strong, hard hands, he started to move, and her only worry was that her legs wouldn't hold her—it all felt so good.

Then he left her body, leaned in close over her shoulder.

"I burn for you, Joanna. But I want to know you want me just as much. Tell me, or I'll stop," he said softly by her ear, making her shiver.

"Please, don't stop..."

"Why?"

"I want you...I *need* you, Ben," she begged, and was willing to do it again, as many times as she needed to, to have him inside her, taking away the ache and the loneliness.

"I need you, too," he said, sinking his teeth lightly into her shoulder as he entered her again, deep and full, not holding back this time as he quickened the pace and sent them both reeling when heat exploded between them.

She started to move away, but he held her in place.

"Again," he panted, and she blinked, realizing he was still hard inside her, and moving again, taking her under.

But Joanna had had enough of him calling the shots, and reached down to turn up the warm water before facing him.

"Let me," she said, looking into his eyes and sliding to her knees before him, watching the water wash over his skin as she dragged her nails down his thighs, then back up before closing over the root of him and taking him into her mouth.

"Oh, Jo," he ground out, pushing a little farther into her, and she welcomed his invasion. "Yessss," he hissed, his hands placed gently on her hair as he helped her set a pace that made him even harder.

She massaged the loose skin around the head of his shaft with her tongue, loving his taste, and how his legs trembled as he approached the edge. With her other hand, she fluttered her fingers over his sac, and slightly behind, massaging the tender stretch of skin that sent him off. Ben's entire body convulsed as he came, emptying himself into her, making her answer his groans of release with her own sounds of satisfaction.

He reached down, hooking his hands under her arms and helping her back up to fuse himself to her in a deep kiss.

When they parted, he pushed her hair back from her face, and looked at her in a way that broke her heart. So tender, so full of…something that was not just about the sex.

"I didn't know what to expect when I walked in here," he said, reaching to turn the water off. "I knew I should leave you alone, but…I couldn't."

They stepped out, and she took the towel he offered her.

"I'm glad," she said simply, unsure what to say.

Wrapping the towel around his waist, he met her eyes in the mirror as she wrapped in hers as well.

"What now?" he asked.

"Nothing has changed, Ben," she said, her voice soft. "I have a job to do, and we can't let this get in the way. And when it's done, I'll be back to work. I won't be here, I'll be…God knows where," she said with a humorless grin. "But I won't be here."

"It would have helped a lot to know that when you showed up here," he said frankly, opening the door as they stepped outside into the darker hall. "But I can't say I'm not glad it happened. And I'd like it to happen again," he added.

Heat rose between them, and she realized she was ready for him again, ready to give herself over to this man in a way she never had for any other.

"Me, too, but you know that once you go to court, you probably won't see me again after that. And if I was smart, I'd walk downstairs right now, call my supervisor, and have him send out someone else. Someone male," she added, making him smile.

"Don't do that, Jo," Ben said, walking forward, backing her against the wall. "Don't go yet. I'll testify, do what I need to do. I'm a big boy. I know we'll be over when it's done. I won't get in the way of you doing your job, or moving on. But at night, here, when we're alone..."

His hands slid up to loosen the towel, letting it fall to the floor.

She gasped as he touched her, convinced her with his hands, his fingers and lips. She clung to him as he lifted her, taking her again as if his life depended on it, his thrusts deep and set into a rhythm her body seemed to know by heart.

How could she say no? They'd part ways soon enough. He'd testify, he'd cooperate, and in the end, she would move on.

"Yes, at night...this," she said breathlessly, kissing him.

Holding on tight, she moved against him, not wanting to let go. Not yet, anyway.

11

BEN KEPT HIS PROMISE. FOR THE next week, they worked the bar, and Joanna watched his back, did her job, as did Marshal Stivers at his parents' ranch.

During the day, they maintained friendly, professional distance, though if he could somehow touch her while passing her a tray, or walking by in the kitchen, he did. He needed to gather up as many touches as he could. She was only his—and only at night—for less than a week.

But the nights were shatteringly hot. Ben knew there was going to be a wicked price to pay after this, but he didn't care, not as long as they were together right now.

The trial didn't bother him as much as thinking about Joanna being gone after it was over. She'd go back to her work and that would be that.

Sure, they could meet up, maybe see each other now and then, but Ben knew he wouldn't—that would never be enough.

He made it through another day, serving beer, chatting with Lisa, joking with Charlie as if nothing was wrong, as if everything was just fine.

By the time they closed up and he and Joanna were heading back to the house, he had a rotten headache, and needed some air.

"Let me check the perimeter before you come out."

"I'll go with you. I need a walk."

She paused, considering, and then nodded.

As they walked to the end of the building, he shoved his hands in his pockets, took a deep breath of evening air.

"Did I ever tell you that your brother called me?"

She stopped short for a moment, looking at him under the starry sky.

"Jarod called you?"

"Yeah. That's not a man you want on the phone asking if you are the bastard who made his sister cry," Ben said with a chuckle. "Other than that, he sounds like a nice guy. Obviously cares for you, a lot."

Joanna shook her head. "I can't believe he did that. I am so going to kick his butt when I see him," she said.

"It's good to know that none of that was true—that he didn't care, wasn't there for you," he said.

"I hated lying about that—Jarod is amazing. And so is my dad. And now I have my sister-in-law…they are all wonderful."

"Family is important. And Lenny…I assume he was fictional, too?"

"Sort of. There was a Lenny in my past, and he was kind of a jerk, but nothing like what I told you. Sorry about that. I had a friend who went through something similar with another guy, so I sort of just worked off partial truths."

"To make believable lies," he noted, nodding. "College?"

"Master's degree in criminal justice," she admitted. "It was where I learned to waitress, too."

"And your brother and father are Texas Rangers," he said. "Your mom?"

"That part was true. She really did take off when I was seven. I have no idea where she is, what she's doing. And I can't say I care. Jarod and Dad are my family."

"So how come you didn't end up a Ranger?"

"The marshals were a good fit for me, and I didn't want anyone saying I had the way paved for me by my family."

"Can't believe they'd dare," he said lightly, making her laugh again. He liked her laugh—it was easy, genuine. "But I know people can make those connections, even when they aren't true. You see Jarod and your dad often?"

"More lately, especially since I was—" She stopped. They hadn't talked about it, though he'd seen the scar. Touched it, kissed it.

"Shot," he supplied softly.

"Yeah, it was—"

"My dad showed me a news article. Showed you being loaded up into an ambulance."

"Oh. I was tracking this guy in Yuma, a real monster who had been evading everyone for a while. His last victim was a fifteen-year-old girl he raped and left for dead. He was arrested, and managed to escape when his transport driver had a heart attack. I had him cornered, but backup was probably at least twenty minutes away. So, I went in. Long story short, I was shot, he took off…it was a mess, basically."

"But they found him?"

"Oh, yeah. The FBI found him a few days later, holed up. I only wish I had had the chance to take him in," she said bitterly.

"Well, what matters is that he's off the streets, and that you survived."

"Barely. Physically and career-wise. I didn't impress anyone for going in on my own, not waiting for backup. The USMS doesn't really care for exposure in front-page news articles, even in small-town newspapers, and the fact that another agency managed to take him down stung, too."

"You did what you had to do," he said.

"Thanks."

"It must have been hard for your family. What about your dad?"

"He's getting close to retirement. Jarod's in administration these days. He took a promotion, got married. They're thinking about starting a family," she said.

It was a little weird, considering how intimate they had been, feeling as though he was just getting to know her. Their nights hadn't been full of conversation lately; they used their precious hours together otherwise.

"That's nice, that he can make that work. Does he miss being out there?"

"Maybe sometimes, but I think he'd miss his wife more."

"It sounds like you all did fine, even with your mom taking off."

"It was hard at first. Dad and Jarod didn't always know what to do with a girl growing up, but they taught me the most important stuff."

"Such as?"

She grinned up at him. "How to shoot, how to drive,

how to read a map, how to be safe in the desert, how to fend off boys."

Ben laughed. "Those would be the top five things teenage girls should know," he agreed, and then he narrowed his eyes on her. "How to shoot, huh? When did you start?"

"Around age seven."

"So you were choking on purpose."

"It wasn't easy, believe me, especially when I know I'm a better shot than you, or at least as good," she said, and he grinned at the challenge in her tone.

"It would be nice to have a chance to find out."

"You'll have to take my word for it, I guess."

"Part of my decision to leave the SEALs had to do with someone getting shot."

"You took a bullet for someone?"

"No. The other way around."

"One of your team died protecting you," she supplied, some things now clicking into place. "Is that why you resisted protection from us so much?"

"Maybe. It's hard to think of anyone else putting their life on the line for you. There was a young guy, new to the team, Tony Lorrano. We were infiltrating a warehouse and the guard was supposed to be clear at the time, but he wasn't. Tony and I were paired up, and I guess he saw the guard before I did, and he stepped in front of me to return fire, but it was too late."

"So you feel guilty for Tony dying, which made you willing to put yourself in front of a bullet in this situation? Some kind of balancing of the scales?"

"I don't think so. I've been running that night over in my head, the night of the shooting," he said. "It's like there's something I can't quite see straight."

"That's normal. Is there something in particular that's bugging you?"

"Just that I can't remember if I reacted quickly enough, the same as what happened with Tony. I've been through situations, training like that, hundreds of times, and I keep wondering if I could have done something to save either of them, Tony or the rodeo official. Why didn't I see it? Why wasn't I fast enough?"

"You could drive yourself crazy with that thinking. You've lost a lot, and I can see how that would make you want to handle things on your own, but if you died, that wouldn't help. Bad men would go free, and your family would have lost you. You can't control it all. You can't save the whole world and make everything right," she said, covering his hand with hers. "Not even big, bad navy SEALs can do that."

"I know," he said, turning his hand over to hold hers. "Or U.S. Marshals," he added with a lifted brow, making her grin.

"Well, maybe." Her smile faded.

Ben leaned in to kiss her ear before he pulled her forward. She stepped aside, looking around.

"Not out here. Never in public, you know that."

He looked around at the sprawl of the desert at their feet, the starry sky.

"This is hardly public," he said.

"You know what I mean. Let's get inside," she said, scanning the horizon, suddenly tense.

"You see something?" he said, also training his own gaze on the landscape around them.

"I don't think so, but we should go," she said. "Standing around out here wasn't a good idea."

She fell in behind him, and it took every ounce of

control he had not to pull her up alongside, or put her in front of him, but she was being his marshal again, not his lover.

It reminded him of the space between them, and that he had been pretending that this was real, when in truth, it was no more real than what they had shared before. Their desire was real, but everything else was temporary.

Inside the house, she blew out a breath, relaxing.

"Stay here—"

"I know, you'll check the place out, and I'll stay here like a good little boy," he said with a forced smile.

"I know it's hard, Ben, but it's almost over."

Like he needed another reminder.

JOANNA WOKE SUDDENLY, BEN'S arm thrown over her, her awareness sharp. Her eyes went to the window, where she heart it again, something down below. A footfall, a snapped twig.

Ben was passed out, snoring, which made her smile a little as he said he didn't snore. She slipped from his embrace very gently so as not to wake him up. Slipping into her jeans and T-shirt, unable to find her shoes in the dark, she went downstairs without them.

She kept the lights off, and went to a window near where she had heard the sound. Someone moved in the shadows, near where her car was parked out back. Walking silently to the door, she slipped out into the dark and locked the door behind her. Reaching for her cell phone, she called Stivers, whispering.

"I might have something here," she said.

"Need me there?" He sounded wide awake.

"Not just yet...let me check it out, but you might

want to take a second look around there, in case we're both getting visitors."

"Will do."

Joanna shoved the phone in her pocket, calmed her breathing, moving silently in bare feet across the rocky, uneven surface of the gravel-covered area in front of the porch.

Putting the possibility of stepping on something poisonous at the back of her mind, she focused on her surroundings, mentally calculating the movement of the shadow she thought she saw, and heading in that direction.

Her thinking quieted, her focus homing in on the sound that seemed to come from around the side of the bar—a scrape or creak of metal, like a door opening. Then again, followed by a clunk of something heavy on metal.

Joanna headed toward the sound, moving quickly until she stopped short, caught in the eyes by the glare of headlights. A second later, a gunshot, and a bullet zipped by her head, making her hit the ground and crawl back behind the corner of the building, where she found…Ben.

"What are you doing here?" she hissed, reaching for her phone to contact Stivers and call for backup.

"I heard you get dressed, go out. I knew something must be up."

"Yes, there is something most definitely up," she said between clenched teeth, and cursed as she heard the engine of a vehicle start up. "And they're getting away."

Making her call, she glared at Ben. "Get back in the house."

"What if that's what they want? What if this is a distraction to lure you away?"

She blew out a breath. "Okay, stay with me, then, but stay low. Whoever it was, they're escaping," she said in exasperation, hearing tires grind over gravel in the parking lot as she raced up the other side of the bar, gun drawn.

Sure enough, the pickup had just made its way to the road, and Joanna knew of only one way to stop it, firing on the vehicle as it hit the gas. She aimed for the back tires, not wanting to risk shooting the driver, if she could help it.

Her aim was dead on, as the tires blew and the pickup went out of control, teetering over the edge of the road into the ditch, half on its side.

"Stop!" she shouted, keeping her gun aimed as she approached the car. "U.S. Marshal. Hold your fire," she shouted.

Joanna heard the door open, saw a figure emerge, the engine still running. She dove behind a rock, searching for cover, but her assailant didn't seem to be interested in shooting now. He was running.

Cursing the lack of shoes again, she took off after him, easily following the sound of the person in front of her breaking through the brush.

Holstering her gun as she got closer, she prepared to take the runner down when another figure lunged from the side, and, for a moment, her heart was in her mouth as she thought: *mountain lion.*

Close.

Taking the flashlight from her pocket, she heard the sound of fist hitting flesh, and shone the light on the two men grappling on the desert floor.

The one on top was clearly Ben. He was restraining the shooter easily, still, Joanna grabbed her gun again, just in case. Then, unexpectedly, Ben almost slammed back into her when he cursed and flung himself backward from the guy on the ground.

His shock matched her own as her flashlight fell on the face of the shooter, illuminating the few feet between them.

"Charlie," they both said in unison, and Joanna felt her abraded feet suddenly starting to ache along with her head.

This was going to be a long night.

JOANNA SAT ON A KITCHEN CHAIR they had dragged into the bathroom on the first floor of Ben's home, muttering while he helped her wash and put antiseptic on her lacerated feet. She hadn't wanted to bother until he pointed out she was leaving bloody, dirty footprints where she walked, not to mention that she was risking infection.

She'd tried to do it herself, but then he'd taken over, and the truth was, he was succeeding better than she. It gave her time to think, and he probably wanted to keep busy as well.

This had been a surprise for both of them, but a far more upsetting one for Ben. If it made it easier for him to tend to her bumps and bruises, she was okay with that.

Charlie was handcuffed to the refrigerator—her call—though he had promised not to run.

Sure.

There was no doubt that he was guilty of some pretty serious charges.

"Let me talk to him first," Ben said quietly, pressing a bandage over a particularly sore scrape.

"No. I have to handle this by the book," she said tightly, trying to ignore how good his hands felt on her bruised and cut foot.

Ben sat back on his heels, packing up the medical supplies from his cabinet and handing her a pair of his clean socks.

"Put those on. They'll be big, but they'll keep your feet clean, maybe see a doctor tomorrow to make sure everything's all right."

Today seemed as though it had been a million years long. An hour, or a bullet or two, could change everything. Tomorrow seemed a long time away.

Joanna knew she had to go out and talk to Charlie—find out who he was working with, and if anyone else was here with him—she couldn't go easy on him because of his relationship with Ben. Or because of her relationship with Ben.

Everything was still a mess, but she was going to play by the rulebook on this.

Her heart was torn. She cared for Ben—what they had was more than sex, yes, as if sex wasn't complicated enough—but she had a job to do, and that job meant, very likely, bringing some very serious charges against Ben's closest friend.

The way she saw it, there was no way for her job not to come between them.

"Listen, I have to go in there, then I'll have to call someone to come get him and take him into San Antonio. You understand that, right?" Marshal Stivers was still on watch at the ranch, and everyone thought it was best he maintain his status there until this was all over with. Nailing Charlie didn't mean there weren't more out there.

She stood, wincing as she tested which foot hurt less, then settled her full weight on to them.

"You need to hear what he has to say first," Ben said, unable to keep the defensiveness out of his tone.

"Sure, but I can't imagine what he can say that will help much. He *shot* at us, Ben," she said. "Or at me, to be specific. He probably set the fire, or he knows who did. What we have to find out is the level of his involvement. If he knows enough maybe he can cut a deal, but he's definitely looking at doing time," she said, putting the hard facts out there as plainly as she could. Sugarcoating it wouldn't help.

Ben stood very still and then nodded, though he didn't get up from where he was sitting.

"I know Charlie like a brother. There has to be some kind of explanation."

Joanna reached out hesitantly, putting a hand on his shoulder, and he paused before covering it with his own.

Her heart ached a little, as it almost seemed like a goodbye of sorts. As she walked out to do what she had to do, he remained behind.

"So Charlie, how long have you been involved in this and who do you work for? That's really what we need to know," Joanna said, sitting at the table and leaving the man shackled to the refrigerator.

He looked miserable. Dirty, his face bruised, and his shirt torn from where Ben had tackled him. He hung his head, not meeting her eyes.

Shame.

Well, at least he could feel it, she thought, trying to shut down any sympathy for the man who made amazing chili and had played solider with Ben as a boy. Charlie had served his country, and lost a leg doing so. He'd also lied to all of them and shot at her.

"You don't understand. I wasn't trying to hurt you, not really," he said.

"The loaded rifle in your backseat says differently. Did you start the fire at the Callahans' as well?"

He nodded miserably, and it became easier to harden her heart to him. How could he do such a thing to people who had taken him in since he was young?

Not that she hadn't seen it before.

"You turn up some names, lead us to some bigger fish, maybe you get a reduced sentence."

His head snapped up. "I didn't commit any crime! Nothing serious, anyway. I knew that fire wouldn't do much damage, and I'm a dead-on shot. If I'd wanted to kill you or Ben, I could've. I was just trying to…scare you. Scare him."

Joanna leveled an impatient look in his direction. "And why would that be, Charlie?"

"I've been trying to find a way to make him not want to testify. The fire at the house seemed to get him moving that way, and then you managed to turn him back to doing it again."

"How inconvenient."

"Yeah. He was on the edge, though, and I figured, if he was worried about you, if he thought anyone would hurt you, then he would back off for sure."

Joanna watched Charlie closely. Nothing in his body language suggested he was lying, but he had more to tell.

"Why would you want Ben to renege on his testimony? Someone paying you off? Did they come to you, or did you go to them? Sell out your best friend for the right price?"

"No!" Charlie objected vehemently.

"Then why?" she asked again, leaning over the table, losing patience.

Awareness prickled at the back of her neck, and she slid a look behind her, noting Ben in the doorway of the kitchen. Charlie hadn't seen him yet.

"They know things about me that…no one else knows. And they said they would hurt Lisa and the kids," he confessed miserably. "As well as Ben."

"What kinds of things?" Joanna asked, not falling for his story.

Charlie looked up then and noticed that Ben had stepped into the room. Joanna stepped around the table.

"Fine, if you won't tell me, it will be easy enough to find out later," she said, pulling out her cell phone to call her office. They'd need to send someone either to cover Ben while she took Charlie in or to take him in themselves.

Either way, she was tired, and it was getting harder to keep her very conflicted emotions under wraps. If she couldn't break Charlie, she knew the marshals at headquarters would find out whatever he was hiding.

"Charlie, is Lisa safe? The kids?" Ben asked, stopping Joanna in her tracks before she dialed.

She caught her breath, realizing she hadn't asked that first, which she should have. She cursed silently, kicking herself.

"I don't know…for the moment, yeah, but if they

find out, if they know I'm busted..." Charlie said. "I don't know what they'll do."

Joanna put her phone down again, reaching for patience and softening her approach. "Enough of this, Charlie. Details, now."

Ben's steadying hand squeezed her shoulder.

"Tell us how you got involved in this, Charlie," he said. "No matter what it is. We need to know everything."

"There was a guy I used to get my drugs from in Houston," Charlie admitted, all of the air seeming to collapse from him.

"You were an addict?" Joanna asked.

"Yeah. Prescription pain killers. After I got out of the VA, I was sort of still messed up. The pain was less than it had been months before, but it was still there, and I started needing more than they'd give me. I started getting what I needed off the street from this guy, Joe, and before I knew it, things were going downhill fast. If it weren't for Ben showing up, giving me a job, I probably would have ended up dead somewhere."

Joanna swung a look to Ben. "You knew about this?"

He put his hands up, looking sincerely shocked. "No. Charlie, why would you hide something like that?"

It was Charlie's turn to look shocked. "How could I let you know I had a habit? How I'd failed? You're the *hero,* not me. I didn't want anyone to know. I haven't used since I came here, I promise you that," Charlie said, eyes on Ben, tears falling openly.

Joanna looked away, gathering her thoughts. This wasn't what she'd expected.

"You could have killed her, Charlie," Ben said flatly.

"One move an inch this way or that, and she could be dead right now."

Joanna looked up, surprised at the level of repressed fury in his voice.

"I wouldn't let that happen," Charlie said adamantly.

"You know it doesn't work that way. You got lucky," Ben said, leaning in. "Someone moves a few inches, and suddenly it's all over. Why didn't you just come to me? About all of it? From the start? We're like brothers. You should have called me the minute you were out of the VA. You should have told me about the threat."

"I know. I went through the therapy, but I still thought I'd never be any use to anyone this way," he said, kicking his fake leg out, as if wanting to send it away from his body. "And I was so afraid for Lisa, for the kids, and that if they found out, they wouldn't want anything else to do with me," Charlie said, sinking to the floor, his arm still attached to the fridge handle.

Ben looked askance at Joanna, and she knew what he wanted, reaching into her pocket and handed him the key to the cuffs. Ben crossed the kitchen and unlocked the cuffs, helping Charlie up.

"You should have trusted me, Charlie. And you have to trust me now, and Joanna. Tell us everything you know, and maybe we can stop this before anything else bad happens."

Joanna tensed as Charlie took a step forward, but it was clear that Charlie wasn't going to hurt Ben, or anybody. The look on his face told her that.

"Let's start with who threatened you and go from there," she said. "Ben, can you call Lisa and have her come here with the kids right away? Don't tell her more than you have to to get her here."

"No, I don't want her to know!" Charlie said loudly, and Joanna turned to face him.

"It's time to deal with the people you've been lying to, Charlie, including Lisa. You put her and her kids, as well as Ben and me, in danger. All so that you could protect your secrets, your hopes and dreams," she said, nailing him with a harsh look. "If you help me, tell me what I need to know, I won't report the shots fired tonight. I believe that you were trying to miss, but you are going to take responsibility for the fire, and you are going to tell Lisa everything."

"But—"

"Shut up, Charlie, and listen to the marshal, or I'll help her haul you in myself," Ben added coolly.

Charlie froze, slowly nodding.

"Okay. Okay..." he agreed, quietly sitting in a kitchen chair.

Joanna was quiet too, meeting Ben's serious look, and offering a quiet thanks. He could have tried to convince her to go easier on Charlie, taken his friend's side against her, made things harder.

He hadn't, and that counted for a lot. It didn't make anything she had to do now any easier, but it helped.

She spent the next two hours taking down Charlie's statement, and the two hours after that sitting with him and Lisa while he told her what he had just told Joanna and Ben.

Lisa, to her credit, held up like Fort Knox. Clearly Charlie had underestimated her, as he had Ben, and he seemed to realize that when she had simply walked to him and wrapped her arms around him, crying and letting him know she would do whatever she had to do to stand by him.

By the time a transport from San Antonio showed up to get Charlie and Lisa and take them to the safe house, Joanna was wrung dry and felt more like a relationship counselor than a law-enforcement officer. Ben had kept his distance, more or less, staying close by, listening, but he hadn't said much since his first appearance in the kitchen. On their way out to the van, Charlie turned to Joanna.

"Am I *really* going to do time?"

She blew out a breath. "I don't know. You would for what happened tonight, but we're going to keep that between us. As far as the USMS is concerned, you're voluntarily turning yourself in, so you'll probably get probation and have to do restitution for the fire, assuming the Callahans press charges. Or who knows, you might walk away from it," she said.

"Why are you doing that for me? Not reporting the shooting?"

She turned to look at him, crossing her arms over her middle and wondering if she was making the right call.

"It's not for you. It's for Lisa and the kids, because if you can straighten your act out, they need you. For whatever reason, she seems willing to stick with you, so who am I to take you away from them? They've lost enough," she responded. "Ben has lost enough, too. You have a chance here, Charlie. Don't blow it again. Or I will come after you myself."

He nodded weakly, but she saw the relief and the promise in his eyes.

You could never outrun yourself at seven, she thought morosely, remembering too keenly what it was like to lose a parent and not wanting Lisa's kids to lose their second chance at having a normal home. She could pretend that didn't influence her thinking, but it did.

If she believed that Charlie was dangerous, truly dangerous, she'd never let it slide. But while he'd made some serious errors in judgment, she had no doubt he had truly thought he was protecting them all, and that he loved Lisa and her kids.

"I will, I swear," he said resolutely. "I know I was wrong, just at the time, I guess…I didn't think they would—"

"You underestimated them. You didn't think Ben or Lisa would stick by you, and you had absolutely no reason to think that about them. They love you. Do you get that?"

He nodded. "Yeah, I do. And I'm going to make it up to them in whatever way I can."

"You can start by staying alive and telling us everything you know about the people who were on your back," Joanna said.

"Time to go," the marshal driving the transport said before anyone else could say anything. Lisa offered Joanna a quick hug before helping her two still-half-asleep children.

"Can you take Patsy?" she asked Charlie, who looked as if he'd just been given a million dollars as he lifted up the little girl and hugged her in.

Joanna, nearly sagging in exhaustion, watched the van pull away.

"You need sleep," Ben said, pulling her into his arms.

She let him. It felt too good to argue about.

"Yeah," she agreed.

She headed for the sofa and jerked back when her

feet left the floor, realizing with a shock that Ben was carrying her toward the stairs.

"What are you doing?" she said, pushing back against his chest.

"You need sleep, and you're going to get it. With me," he said simply. "No way are you staying on the couch."

She should argue, Joanna thought as they climbed the steps. It was ridiculous, him carrying her like this. Her feet weren't that sore; she could walk just fine.

Again, she didn't argue. She didn't resist when he took her gun and badge and put them on the table by his massive bed, or when he helped her out of her dusty, dirty clothes, or when he stripped down to his Skivvies and crawled in beside her.

Pulling a quilt up over them both, he hooked an arm around her waist and drew her back against him. He was warm, solid and safe.

It was all that mattered for the moment. She snuggled back in and let herself relax. Ben was already snoring, and it wasn't long before she gave in and joined him.

12

BEN WOKE UP IN THE MIDDLE OF the night, surprised at first by the warm female body snuggled up against his, and then he remembered bringing Joanna to bed with him.

Leaning forward to nuzzle his face into her hair, he thought about the events of the night before, and found he was just as interested in getting to know this new Joanna. Joanna the marshal and Joanna the woman who was pressing her amazing backside against him in a very alluring way.

Learning the truth about her had thrown him, but now it made her all the more intriguing, and the reason for his attraction to her became clear. He had sensed her strength, her focus and her ability all along, even though she had tried to mask them.

His father had said he'd finally found his match, and Ben believed his dad was right.

But she wasn't here for the long haul. She had a job to do, a life to return to, he remembered, with a twist in his gut. It didn't feel right to try to convince her to stay, but it didn't feel right to let her go, either.

What felt right at the moment was touching her.

Sliding an arm around her waist, he nuzzled in closer and kissed the back of her neck, making her arch back more deeply against him. She turned over, facing him.

"You okay?" she asked sleepily, but he was glad she was awake.

"Yeah, I'm good," he said, kissing her softly. With all that had happened before this, he felt as though now was their first time together, with no lies between them. It upped the emotional intensity, because Ben knew now that what was happening here was real. It wasn't a fling.

He wanted to be with Joanna Wyatt.

Her arms linked around him and she was kissing him back. The world and thinking faded to the background as his hands busily disposed of the few scraps she wore, and she did the same for him.

When he pressed her breasts together and drew both aroused nipples into his mouth, her fingers found his shaft and began to stroke him. He lost himself in her scent, her taste.

He was shaking, too, when he lifted up and trailed kisses down her stomach, parting her thighs and dipping down for a kiss. She completely turned him on when her thighs clamped down on his shoulders and she ground against him, taking more.

This was the real Joanna. Hot, passionate and strong. His Joanna. They were both lying to themselves if they thought differently.

His hands steadied her by sliding beneath her backside, massaging her bottom as he continued that slow press with his tongue. She gasped in pleasure, riding it out. He didn't let up until she had come back down again, slack under his hands.

He didn't know what was going to happen when the sun came up, but they were here now, and he wasn't going to worry about it. One way or another, no matter what happened, Joanna was part of his life now. Part of him.

They had the night to play, to explore.

He lifted up over her, and, to his surprise, her hand planted itself on his chest and she pushed him back up against the headboard to a sitting position. Ben shifted as she straddled him, crossing her long legs behind him and enveloping him inside her body, both of them wordless but gasping as she did.

The position kept him deep, very deep, and pleasure subsumed him. She wrapped her arms around him, too, riding him in a slow, seductive grind.

He slid his hands down to her hips, grasping her gently and moving her in a slow, circular motion as he took her lips in a deep kiss, their tongues mating in the same way their bodies were. It was unbearably intimate, wrapped around each other, so deeply connected, and his pounding heart slowed down to a drugging beat as he dipped down to suck at a beaded nipple, making her moan in a completely beautiful way, her head dropping forward to his shoulder.

She tightened her wrapped legs to bring him even deeper and they kept up the motion that was so perfect he wasn't sure he had ever experienced anything like it. Joanna framed his face in her hands, kissed him as he looked at the woman who drove him crazy and pushed his buttons, tempting him and making him feel more than anyone ever had, or he suspected, ever could.

The kiss deepened as she levered her hips to help him hold her up, thrusting her gently against him. Their sighs and moans of mutual release shattered them both in a cascade of sparks and warmth that made him feel as if they had melted together.

One.

That was definitely new. Ben had never really realized it before, but he had always maintained some distance from his lovers—he felt desire, affection, sometimes friendship for them—but never this incredible intimacy that made him hers for good.

JOANNA WATCHED BEN SNOOZE, worn out after their lovemaking—which was what it was. Not sex now, but something more.

She knew what had happened between them tonight wasn't like the other times. This had been…deep.

They'd been wrapped around each other so tightly… she had never been that close with a man. The way he had looked at her when he was deep inside her, everything open to each other, had moved her. In spite of the deceptions between them, she couldn't help but feel that he was one of the only people who truly *knew* her. Then it occurred to her that she had shared more with Ben Callahan than she ever had with anyone—the lies were small details, but everything else they shared was true.

She drew her fingers over his cheek, his jaw, to his chest, and felt his hand tighten on her hip, pulling her against him to where he was responding to her, erect in his sleepy state.

Peering over his shoulder, she saw her marshal's star on his nightstand, next to her gun. Joanna had no idea what was coming next, but the idea of being without Ben, of him not being involved in her life, was quickly becoming unbearable.

And that was a problem. She saw women give up their careers, everything they had worked for, for a man, for kids, and regret it. She hadn't devoted her life to her work for this long only to walk away.

She groaned out loud in frustration, unable to find a solution. She couldn't make any guarantees with the way her life was. Work had to come first.

Rubbing his face against her skin, his lips met the scar on her shoulder, making her startle slightly.

"I want to kill the guy myself for doing this to you," he whispered, darting his tongue out against the puckered skin.

She hadn't realized he was awake, watching her.

"He's in jail, where he will rot for the rest of his life. Don't worry about it."

"I hate the idea of anyone hurting you," he said.

She smiled in the dark. Normally, a man saying that would irritate her to no end, but having Ben feel so protective of her made her warm inside.

"No worries, cowboy," she said, lightening the moment. "I can handle myself, and you too."

"Don't I know it," he said with a smile in his voice before he continued to kiss her, her breasts, her stomach and lower again.

He erased any thoughts for several minutes, and Joanna was sure she'd never experienced such luxurious pleasure with a lover before.

So maybe they could just have what they had right now, she thought. They'd enjoy this, and deal with the rest later.

She sighed as he lifted over her and she parted her thighs, allowing him to settle in between. He didn't accept her invitation just yet, but planted soft kisses on her neck, making her moan sleepily and push back a little more insistently.

Finally, just when she was about to get bossy, he slid inside and gave her what she needed. All of him, as deep as he could be and pushing deeper still.

"More," was all she could say, opening wider and linking her legs around his hips, her hands grasping his shoulders tightly.

He pumped his hips faster, harder, turned on by the gasps and whimpers of pleasure that she couldn't hold back as she reached a hand down to touch him where his body met hers, and then herself.

"Harder," she cried, wanting him to lose it completely, to take her in the way she had fantasized about since they'd met.

He pulled away, and to her pleased surprise, flipped her over so she could push up on all fours. He was back inside her instantly, holding her hips as she held on to the headboard to steady herself against the motion.

Yes, this is what she wanted. All-out, nothing held back, she thrust back against him so hard that she thought they might fall off the bed. She'd never been more turned on in her life.

"I—I can't hold on, Jo," he said, his breathing heavy.

"I know," she panted, feeling delectably feline, like the tiger on her hip, loving how she could make her man lose his iron-clad control. She was just as close to the edge. "Me too."

Ben hammered into her relentlessly, shouting her name as an orgasm wracked his body, emptying him out as Joanna cried out from her own climax a split second later.

Both of them collapsed back to the bed, breathing heavily, their limbs tangled together as they recovered. When his fingers found hers, quietly linking, Joanna knew what she'd known all along: she was in love with Ben Callahan.

Stemming the burn of tears, she waited until he was sleeping, then slid from the bed. Finding her clothes, she took her phone, gun and badge, and closed the bedroom door quietly behind her.

BEN AWOKE ALONE AND AT FIRST he was disappointed to reach for Joanna and find her side of the bed empty, but then he settled back, relieved to have a moment to himself. She was probably downstairs on watch, doing what she did. What had happened between them both times tonight was off the scales, both in terms of being the hottest sex he'd ever had, and because he was experiencing such intense emotions about it. Their time together had been far from normal, certainly, and it was all moving fast, but Ben knew what he was feeling, and that it was real.

He loved Joanna Wyatt, and he had to find a way to convince her to give what they had a chance.

Smiling, he thought about the week until the trial—he had that much time to convince her, and he looked forward to trying.

Taking a quick shower, he smiled at the amazing aroma wafting up from the kitchen and figured Joanna had made some breakfast. He threw on some sweats and a T-shirt, heading downstairs.

Turning the corner of the kitchen with a wide smile,

he found himself anticipating seeing her even though she had been with him all night.

Things were different now. He had a plan, hopes for the future.

"Hey, lover, whatever you're cooking, it smells amazing—"

He stopped short when he didn't find Joanna at the kitchen counter, but a tall, powerful-looking man who slanted a grin his way.

"Sorry to disappoint, but glad you like my grandma's waffle recipe," the guy said, and then held out a hand, the badge hanging around his neck telling Ben all he needed to know. "Marshal Russ Tyler. Grab a plate," he said congenially, and headed to the table with a plate of his own.

"Where's Jo…Marshal Wyatt?"

The guy shrugged. "Don't know the details, but I was called in to replace her and so you're stuck with me for the week. Joanna was called back to San Antonio early this morning, and it must have been important, since they hauled me out of bed to get here right away," Tyler explained. "She didn't tell me anything, just took off out of here like her ass was on fire."

Ben leaned back against the counter, shocked. Dismayed. Then concern set in.

"Did something happen with Charlie? The witness they took in from here last night?"

Again the marshal shrugged and continued with his breakfast.

Ben grabbed his phone, dialed Joanna's number, and waited. It went to voice mail.

He tried again.

"Sit down and eat. Most likely, they decided to take

her off WITSEC and put her on fugitive pursuit. I heard something about a prison break over at Telford, and they probably needed her on that more," he added.

A prison break? Ben's blood ran cold thinking about her involved in something like that, but that was her life, wasn't it? And she'd gone back to it without so much as waking him up for a kiss goodbye.

The ache he felt threatened to collapse his chest, but he managed to hold himself upright, grabbing some breakfast, moving mechanically to the table. He was numb, and couldn't quite process all of the strong emotions running through him. Love, worry, anger, shock.

The waffles that had smelled so good a few minutes ago now tasted like cardboard.

"It happens," Tyler said, watching him closely.

"What?"

"Sometimes lines are crossed, people mix it up, and someone always gets hurt. Better she left. Ones like her, they have to run, they aren't good at staying put," he said, almost kindly.

"You know her?"

"In passing, but that's my point. Some of the marshals, especially in fugitive pursuit, they live for the chase. Once they catch you, well, it's time to move on," he said, slanting that smile again.

Ben wanted to hit him, but knew he was probably right. What did he expect? That Joanna would give up her career and stay here with him, waiting tables for the rest of her life?

He'd been a fool.

"I have only one concern," Tyler said.

"What's that?"

"If that affects your willingness to testify."

Ben thought about it, but the answer was easy. Even without Joanna here, he had to do the right thing. "Yeah, I'll be in court."

"Good. Don't worry. Putting those guys away will make you feel a lot better."

Ben wasn't sure that was true, but he nodded. Even so, he was pretty sure that he wouldn't feel better for a good, long while.

13

A WEEK AFTER SHE HAD LEFT Ben's in the middle of the night, Joanna paced the courtroom in San Antonio where Ben was to give his testimony against the rodeo judge's killer. She was there in a completely unofficial capacity, unable to stay away, waiting for the other marshals to escort him out. Then he would be finished with his obligation. This trial, however, was only to put the killer of the rodeo official away—for life.

Charlie's testimony, with that of his former dealer, Joe, was the key to putting the bigger bad guys away for a good long time. After they had agreed to be witnesses, the U.S. Attorney no longer needed Ben's testimony to pressure the killer into spilling, and that made Ben a whole lot safer—and happier, Joanna figured. He'd never been easy with his testimony being used to leverage a deal with a killer who would be free, then protected by WITSEC. Instead, they were all going to jail.

Charlie's testimony, paired with that of his former drug dealer, Joe, unraveled the entire operation. It meant Charlie could be a target for the rest of his life, and so he had been offered a deal. New location, new identity. Full WITSEC rollout. Joe, as well.

He hadn't given them his decision yet, knowing it meant leaving everything behind.

Joanna jumped as the court doors behind her opened, the soft swish echoing in the empty hall. She turned, disappointed to see it was only Don, her supervisor, leaving the courtroom.

"You seem on edge, Marshal," he said, his lips twitching in a smile. "You'd think you were out here waiting for someone."

"Funny, Don. You're a really funny guy," she said flatly. "How is he doing? Did he testify yet?"

"In a few minutes."

"I wish I could go in and see him."

"It's probably better you don't. Don't want him losing his focus."

"Yeah. You're right."

Don had taken the news about her and Ben surprisingly well—and had commended her for making the smart move the week before the trial. It had gone a long way in cementing his faith in her readiness to return to full duty. Which was ironic, since she was thinking of not returning to her job; not in fugitive pursuit, anyway.

A week without Ben had been torture. He'd called her a few times, and it had taken every ounce of self-control she had not to answer.

She didn't know which was worse.

"Listen, there's something else I wanted to talk to you about," she added, grabbing his elbow before he went in.

"Now?"

"Well, just to let you know, I'd like to be permanently reassigned to WITSEC in San Antonio, if possible. I know I've always said it's not for me, but…things change."

"Sudden urge to stay local, huh?"

"Something like that. I'm tired of chasing lowlifes all over the planet."

"Never thought I'd see the day, but I think we can work something out," Don said with an amused smirk.

He turned to walk into the courtroom, and she grabbed him one more time.

"Oh, something else," she said.

He turned, leveling her a look, hands on hips. "What?"

"The file on Lisa's husband…can we do something about that?"

"Already done. She'll have her divorce by the end of the week, and we're putting through paperwork to relocate her, Charlie and the kids. He said he'd go if she goes with him."

Joanna smiled in relief. It wouldn't be easy for them, leaving everything they knew, or for those they left behind, but she knew that WITSEC could provide some communication, maybe even a chance for Ben and Charlie to get together in the future. Especially if she was in charge of their case, but she figured she'd float that idea by Don another day.

"We'll talk more when this is over," he said.

As Don went into the courtroom, Joanna continued to pace the hallway, thinking she should leave and approach Ben another time, but she couldn't quite make herself do it.

It had been wrong, leaving like that, not explaining, but she'd been afraid he would talk her into staying.

One kiss, and she would have been back in his bed. She'd had to go, do the right thing. He needed a marshal who could keep him safe, and she'd needed to get her head on straight.

As it turned out, it was her heart that made her finally know what she had to do.

It was the first time she would be seeing Ben in a week. Her hands were actually clammy as she waited for him to exit the courtroom.

As Ben was ushered out of the back of the courtroom, she found her way to where they would take him to the transport. She released a long breath as they emerged, and froze to the spot, watching.

He was dressed in a formal suit, more polished than she had ever seen him. He looked good enough to eat.

Marshals escorted him out of court, and she finally found the courage to speak up, her throat hoarse and dry.

"Ben," she called, or more accurately, croaked.

Luckily the marshals with him knew who she was and didn't shoot her, but they did stand watching with broad grins, and Joanna knew there was going to be no end to the guff she was going to take for this. Apparently, it was common knowledge she'd fallen for her witness.

And she couldn't care less.

"It's good to see you," she said, coming forward and looking up into Ben's face.

He seemed surprised, then guarded, and nodded. "You, too."

Talk about awkward silence. Joanna decided to break it.

"Um, I know I left in a hurry, and I should explain about that."

"No need. I get it."

"I don't think you..." She stopped talking and did what she'd been dying to do, taking his face in her hands and kissing him.

The marshals beside them cleared their throats.

Breaking the kiss, she waved them off.

"You can beat it, guys. I'll take it from here," she said, staring into Ben's deep honey-colored eyes, and hardly aware of anything else.

"I CAN MAKE IT TO MY CAR ON my own," he said coldly as Joanna followed him out of the building. "They were only seeing me there as a formality, I guess. They do it with all witnesses, until they are clear of the building. I don't need protection anymore, since—"

"I know. I know about Charlie, and how it all worked out. I'm so glad, for him, Lisa, and for you," she said honestly.

Ben was pretty sure the last week had been the longest one of his life, but the minute he'd seen Joanna standing there, it had all evaporated. He'd been glad his testimony was over quickly, the defense having no interest in cross-examining him evidently. When he'd walked out of court, he'd been relieved, and thought it was over.

Then she was there, bringing it all back.

She was breathtaking, even in the somewhat shapeless blue blazer she wore with her jeans, her badge hanging around her neck. There were shadows under her eyes, as if she had slept about as little as he had.

"Tyler said you had been called back to fugitive

pursuit. Something about a prison break? Catch your man?" he asked lightly, trying to make this casual, as if his heart wasn't slamming so hard it might break ribs.

"Not quite yet," she said under her breath. "I wasn't called away for the break. I left because that night, when we were together, it was too intense. I was in too deep, and I knew if I didn't leave then, I might never leave."

"Oh," he said on a breath. "So you just…left. And didn't answer my calls."

He'd comforted himself somewhat with the notion that she had been called back, that it was important, an emergency, and that she hadn't been able to get back in contact with him. He guessed that was a pipe dream, too. So why was she here?

"I know," she said, obviously stressed, pushing her hand through her long, silky hair in the way she always did when she was agitated. "I know that was…cold. But I panicked. I'd never thought I was in love before, and it was under the worst possible circumstances. I had to get away, to think," she said, and he stopped in his tracks by the car, staring at her.

"You thought you were in love?"

Melted-chocolate eyes lifted to his, looking more uncertain than he had ever seen her look.

"Yeah. I know I shouldn't have bolted, and I'm sorry for that, but…I love you. I knew it that night, and I knew it all week, when I missed you so much I wasn't worth crap to anyone."

"You love me?" he repeated, feeling a little stunned at the revelation, and not sure how it affected the tangle of thoughts and emotions raging inside of him.

She'd left him high and dry because she loved him?

"Yes, I love you," she said again, hands on hips, looking even more aggravated. "So there, I said it. And I know you're probably really ticked at me, first for lying to you, then for leaving, and I know you probably don't feel the same way, but I needed to say it, at least, and—"

"I love you, too," he said, stopping the tirade.

She was impossibly gorgeous, the slight breeze teasing her hair against the smooth skin of her neck, and the softness of her mouth, "Let's go sit," he said as she stared at him in clear surprise. Taking her hand, they made their way to a bench in the shade of a tree.

"I asked Don about joining WITSEC on a permanent basis. He seemed to think it was a possibility," she blurted, clearly apprehensive about his response, though he wondered why. He'd certainly never expected her to quit her job, and wondered if she had thought that he did. He'd left the military because it was the right choice for him; it had been time.

It wasn't time for Joanna yet, and maybe it never would be. She loved what she did, and he was fine with that.

"I thought you didn't like working Witness Protection."

She grinned. "You could say it's grown on me."

"I see." He smiled back.

"I would be working out of the San Antonio office, and I'd probably have a heavy caseload, but I'd be here. It can be a demanding schedule, but I'd be here, not chasing criminals all over the country," she said.

"That's good. That's really good," he replied, lifting her fingers to his lips. "Would you live in San Antonio, too?"

"I'd have to get a place, yeah. I don't have one now."

"Yes, you do," he said, and she smiled, knowing he meant his house.

"That would be a long drive to work every day," she said. "But I could be out on the ranch every weekend, and maybe I could work something out with Don. Maybe eventually I might ask to go into instruction, probably in firearms. Not now, but later," she said.

"I could see you doing that, when you're ready," he said, hope blossoming between them as they sat, the hurt of the past weeks all but erased. *What was the point of holding on to it?* he thought. She was here now and she loved him.

"I could spend a few days in the city during the week, once I get some new help and an assistant manager at the bar," he offered.

"You'd do that?" she said.

"I'll do whatever it takes to be with you, Joanna. I'm crazy in love with you."

"I'm crazy in love with you, too," she said, and he was quite certain he would never get enough of hearing that, or of saying it back.

They were quiet for a few moments, and he finally stood up, putting his hand out.

"Maybe we can find somewhere more private to continue this discussion," he said, desire flaring as he looked down at her.

"Not me. I'm living with my brother for now, until I get an apartment," she said ruefully.

"I can hold on to the hotel room for a few more days. I can wait a little before heading back to the bar," he said. "Come stay with me. We have catching up to do."

She laughed. "I don't have my bags or a change of

clothes, and technically, I'm still on the clock for another hour."

"Meet me there after you're done, then. Get your bags, but don't worry about bringing much. You won't need it," he said mischievously, making her laugh.

"I'm sure Don won't care—he can page me if he needs me," she said, leaning in to kiss him. "But maybe I'll take a few more of the vacation days coming to me. You can come over to the house, meet my brother," she said with a grin.

Ben grinned, too. He should have known that when Joanna jumped, she jumped all the way. But she knew his family, and he wanted to know hers.

"Does he still want to shoot me?"

"Only a little, but I'm sure we can change his mind. Though we have more important things to attend to first," she agreed, her own eyes darkening as her gaze fell to his lips.

"Good to know you have your priorities straight," he said, laughing, and pulled her in close for a hot kiss. She tasted like heaven, and he didn't let her speak again for several minutes. When they parted, they were breathing heavily, needing more.

"Yes. Finally," she said softly, with a smile before leaning in for another kiss.

"Forever," he said, agreeing, accepting her kiss and happy to leave it at that.

* * * * *

PASSION

For a spicier, decidedly hotter read—
this is your destination for romance!

COMING NEXT MONTH
AVAILABLE JANUARY 31, 2012

#663 ONCE UPON A VALENTINE
Bedtime Stories
Stephanie Bond, Leslie Kelly, Michelle Rowen

#664 THE KEEPER
Men Out of Uniform
Rhonda Nelson

#665 CHOOSE ME
It's Trading Men!
Jo Leigh

#666 SEX, LIES AND VALENTINES
Undercover Operatives
Tawny Weber

#667 BRING IT ON
Island Nights
Kira Sinclair

#668 THE PLAYER'S CLUB: LINCOLN
The Player's Club
Cathy Yardley

You can find more information on upcoming Harlequin® titles, free excerpts and more at www.HarlequinInsideRomance.com.

Louisa Morgan loves being around children. So when she has the opportunity to tutor bedridden Ellie, she's determined to bring joy back into the motherless girl's world. Can she also help Ellie's father open his heart again? Read on for a sneak peek of

THE COWBOY FATHER

by Linda Ford,
available February 2012 from Love Inspired Historical.

Why had Louisa thought she could do this job? A bubble of self-pity whispered she was totally useless, but Louisa ignored it. She wasn't useless. She could help Ellie if the child allowed it.

Emmet walked her out, waiting until they were out of earshot to speak. "I sense you and Ellie are not getting along."

"Ellie has lost her freedom. On top of that, everything is new. Familiar things are gone. Her only defense is to exert what little independence she has left. I believe she will soon tire of it and find there are more enjoyable ways to pass the time."

He looked doubtful. Louisa feared he would tell her not to return. But after several seconds' consideration, he sighed heavily. "You're right about one thing. She's lost everything. She can hardly be blamed for feeling out of sorts."

"She hasn't lost everything, though." Her words were quiet, coming from a place full of certainty that Emmet was more than enough for this child. "She has you."

"She'll always have me. As long as I live." He clenched his fists. "And I fully intend to raise her in such a way that even if something happened to me, she would never feel like I was gone. I'd be in her thoughts and in her actions every day."

Peace filled Louisa. "Exactly what my father did."

Their gazes connected, forged a single thought about fathers and daughters…how each needed the other. How sweet the relationship was.

Louisa tipped her head away first. "I'll see you tomorrow."

Emmet nodded. "Until tomorrow then."

She climbed behind the wheel of their automobile and turned toward home. She admired Emmet's devotion to his child. It reminded her of the love her own father had lavished on Louisa and her sisters. Louisa smiled as fond memories of her father filled her thoughts. Ellie was a fortunate child to know such love.

Louisa understands what both father and daughter are going through. Will her compassion help them heal—and form a new family? Find out in
THE COWBOY FATHER
by Linda Ford, available February 14, 2012.

SHLIHEXP0212